She was amazed at his arrogance

"I don't go to lunch until twelve-thirty," she told him haughtily.

"Are you the boss?"

"Maybe I don't want to have lunch with you, Mr. Thornton."

Amusement lighted his eyes. "This is business, Natalie," he said. "You surely didn't think I was about to demand those 'fringe benefits' right now?" he taunted.

She drew in an angry breath. "There are no fringe benefits!"

Adam pursed his lips thoughtfully. "Then maybe I should think of a few I might like from you."

Natalie couldn't believe this was happening. Adam Thornton was actually flirting with her! "You can think in vain, Mr. Thornton," she said stiffly. "All you'll get from this agency—from me," she added pointedly, "is efficiency."

"It will do for the moment," he shrugged.

CAROLE MORTIMER
is also the author of these

Harlequin Presents

340—SAVAGE INTERLUDE
352—THE TEMPESTUOUS FLAME
365—DECEIT OF A PAGAN
377—FEAR OF LOVE
383—YESTERDAY'S SCARS
388—ENGAGED TO JARROD STONE
406—BRAND OF POSSESSION
418—THE FLAME OF DESIRE
423—LIVING TOGETHER
430—DEVIL LOVER
437—ICE IN HIS VEINS
443—FIRST LOVE, LAST LOVE
452—SATAN'S MASTER
473—FREEDOM TO LOVE
479—POINT OF NO RETURN
502—ONLY LOVER
510—LOVE'S DUEL
518—BURNING OBSESSION
522—RED ROSE FOR LOVE
531—SHADOWED STRANGER
539—FORGOTTEN LOVER
547—FORBIDDEN SURRENDER
556—ELUSIVE LOVER
564—PASSION FROM THE PAST
571—PERFECT PARTNER
579—GOLDEN FEVER
587—HIDDEN LOVE
594—LOVE'S ONLY DECEPTION
603—CAPTIVE LOVING

Many of these titles are available at your local bookseller.

For a free catalog listing all available Harlequin Romances and Harlequin Presents, send your name and address to:

HARLEQUIN READER SERVICE
1440 South Priest Drive, Tempe, AZ 85281
Canadian address: Stratford, Ontario N5A 6W2

CAROLE MORTIMER

fantasy girl

Harlequin Books

TORONTO • NEW YORK • LOS ANGELES • LONDON
AMSTERDAM • PARIS • SYDNEY • HAMBURG
STOCKHOLM • ATHENS • TOKYO • MILAN

For Nan

———————————————————

Harlequin Presents first edition July 1983
ISBN 0-373-10611-4

Original hardcover edition published in 1983
by Mills & Boon Limited

CHAPTER ONE

NATALIE picked up the green receiver as the telephone began to ring on her desk, pushing some of the clutter out of the way to continue making notes on her pad as she took the call. These figures for the Jackson account just couldn't wait, not if she wanted to get the bill paid and her own outstanding debts dealt with at the end of the month.

Consequently her response into the telephone receiver was a little distracted. But not for long!

'Natalie Faulkner?' The husky voice on the other end of the line was definitely male—and definitely angry! It was a voice that put over a wealth of authority and command in just the sound of her name.

Perhaps Natalie should have heeded that tone, but she was still preoccupied with balancing the figures on this account so that it at least looked reasonably correct. Oh dear, she was hopeless at figures. But Dee, her secretary and general assistant—another name for general dogsbody!—had too much to do in the office already, without the added burden of accounts.

'Yes?' she replied vaguely.

'Miss Faulkner,' the voice was icy now. 'You may have time on your hands to waste, but I can assure you I don't,' the man rasped. 'I had to rearrange my schedule this morning to fit in your appointment, the least you could have done was turn up here on time.'

To say she was taken aback was an understatement— she was astounded! Just who did this man think he was, that he could call her like this to rant and rave about an appointment they didn't even have? Her morning was free, she had made sure of that last night before leaving the office, the model agency she ran from this two-roomed office in an ultra-modern office block, the brown-shaded windows giving the building an added elegance from outside. She had checked on her morning being free simply because she knew she had to make the time to deal with the accounts; her own bills had to be paid, not least of them being the rent and upkeep of this office.

Style, that was what she had been told she needed to open an agency like this—the sort of agency that had the best models, the sort of agency that would attract the best clients in town. And style she had here, with the white and silver furniture in both offices, the comfortably white leather chairs for clients, the more practical chair behind her desk in the same soft white leather, the lush green tropical plants that were arranged about the room in abundance. It was all designed to give the impression of wealth and elegance—and it cost her a small fortune.

She could certainly do without complete strangers—for she didn't know this man, would have remembered that cold grating voice if she had ever heard it before—calling her up to tell her she had a non-existent appointment with them.

Still, she was in business, and maybe this man was a prospective client. She never turned away customers. 'I think there must have been some sort of mistake,' she began in a placating voice.

'If there has,' he ground out, 'you made it. Now, with a great deal of more rescheduling I can give you fifteen minutes in an hour's time. Be here!'

'But——'

'I'm not accustomed to repeating myself, Miss Faulkner,' he rasped in that husky voice. 'I explained to your secretary last night that it was urgent I speak to you, and that hasn't changed.'

Dee! Dee had made the appointment after she had left last night—and she had forgotten to tell her. Natalie found the brown appointment book buried beneath the papers on her desk, found the appropriate day, groaning inwardly as she saw the name written down next to ten o'clock. Adam Thornton! That was all she needed. Her most valued client to date and she had missed her one and only appointment with the head of Thornton Cosmetics and Beauty Aids!

She had hardly been able to believe her luck when Jason Dillman, the head of Thornton Cosmetics and Beauty Aids advertising department, had got in touch with her about a Beauty Girl for the new brand of make-up they were introducing. Natalie had been running the agency for about a year, and had enough work to keep ticking over, but the T.C.B.A. contract had been a real feather in her cap, and for the past six months she had been working closely with Jason Dillman supplying the Beauty Girl and other models they needed for their advertising. It was a lucrative contract, even after the models had been paid, and not one she wanted to lose.

'I'm sorry, Mr Thornton,' she was aware of sounding breathless, 'there seems to have been a mix-up this end. I would be pleased to come and see you at eleven-thirty.'

'Very well,' he agreed abruptly, and rang off.

The clatter of the receiver landing in its cradle resounded in her ear, and she slowly put her receiver down. Not a very auspicious beginning to her first meeting with the head of T.C.B.A.! She had known Adam Thornton headed his own company, had even heard Jason Dillman talk of him, but so far she had only dealt with the other man; her role in their advertising was obviously not big enough to attract the attention of the most wealthy man in cosmetics in the country today.

Maybe the successful launching of Beauty Girl, one of her own models, had changed all that? Maybe she was to receive verbal thanks from Adam Thornton himself for finding him exactly the right girl. And there could be no doubting Judith's success, her photograph displaying the new make-up was appearing everywhere at the moment. And yet Natalie didn't think that could be it, not when he had sounded so angry. Of course, that could have just been because she hadn't turned up when he had decided to give her an audience, and yet she didn't think that was it either. Something appeared to be very wrong, and she only hoped she could smooth it over. She really couldn't afford to lose the Thornton contract, for prestigious reasons as much as any other. Business had doubled at the agency since Judith had become Beauty Girl.

She stood up, pacing the room, listening for the return of Dee to the outer office; the older woman had gone down to the central copy room to photo-copy several reports. Poor Dee was rushed off her feet too, Natalie knew that, and normally an important appointment such as the one with Adam Thornton would not have slipped her mind.

A frown marred her brow as she continued to pace the room, the accounts forgotten, beautiful enough to have been a model herself, her hair a gleaming black bob framing her face, her skin like magnolia, her eyes neither blue nor green but somewhere in between— aquamarine, some people said, her black lashes long and thick, her nose short and straight, the perfect bow of her mouth painted a vivid red, emphasising its sensual fullness. In fact, she had been a model for a time, but the work didn't really appeal to her; it didn't offer enough of a challenge. Well, she had a challenge now, and with one of the most powerful men in the world of cosmetics. Her whole agency could depend on how she put herself over at this meeting.

She checked her appearance in the mirrors that covered all of one wall of her office, making the room appear larger than it actually was and giving an appearance of brightness. Natalie looked as calm and composed as ever, evidence of her model's training, her figure was slender, although it gave a totally feminine look to the cream tailored suit she wore with the soft black silky blouse, her legs were long and shapely. Yes, she could undoubtedly still go back to modelling if she needed to—but she didn't want to. She hadn't liked being used as a glamorous clothes-peg.

She was probably overreacting to the call, it was probably just to discuss Beauty Girl with her, as she had first thought.

She checked her own make-up, the dark shadow on her lids, only the vaguest hint of mascara to her naturally dark lashes, the light foundation to her already flawless complexion, a dark blusher to her high cheekbones, the vivid red lip-gloss to her slightly pouting mouth. The latter needed retouching, and she had just finished doing so when she heard Dee return to her office. Thank goodness, she would have to start for Adam Thornton's office very soon.

'Whew!' Dee put the almost glossy sheets in a disorganised pile on her desk. 'That damned machine broke down again,' she wailed, explaining why she had been gone so long. 'It's going to take me for ever to get these into any sort of order!'

Natalie could sympathise with the other woman, having experienced the photocopier for herself. 'I have to go out, Dee,' she said softly. 'To see Mr Thornton.'

'Okay, I'll just—Oh, no, Mr Thornton!' Dee turned to her with a stricken face. She was a small blonde woman, very pretty, with a wonderful taste in clothes, the rich rust of her blouse and trousers suiting her perfectly. 'Oh, Natalie!' she groaned, closing her

sparkling blue eyes in remorse. 'I completely forgot! He
called just as I was leaving last night, and I wrote it
down quickly in your appointment book. Tom has this
wretched 'flu bug,' she spoke of her husband. 'And
what with running around after him all evening, and
then——'

'Hey, calm down!' Natalie smiled. 'No harm done,'
she understated what could turn out to be very
awkward for her. 'We've just made an appointment for
later instead.'

'I hope it's nothing to do with Judith,' Dee frowned.
'She missed another photographic session this morning.'

'Oh no!' Natalie groaned. Judith's tantrums were the
last thing she wanted to cope with this morning, not on
top of everything else.

When Jason Dillman told her Judith had been the
one chosen as Beauty Girl she had been a little worried
about her unreliability, but he had insisted no one else
would do, that it was a direct order from Adam
Thornton himself. She couldn't argue with that.

Dee nodded. 'Jake called this morning, but you were
so engrossed in your accounts it seemed a shame to
disturb you. I called Judith's flat, but there was no
answer.' She shrugged. 'It's far from the first time she's
done this.'

'I know,' Natalie acknowledged, chewing on her
bottom lip. 'Judith's turning out to be a problem.' And
she could be the reason Adam Thornton wanted to see
her after all, but not for a pat on the back!

'She's always been a problem,' Dee dismissed, sitting
down to begin sorting the sheets into order. 'And I
warned you about letting her become Beauty Girl.'

Natalie didn't mind the criticism. She and Dee had
struck up a very close working relationship in the
eighteen months they had been together, and that was

the way it should be. With only the two of them
running this agency they very often had to more or less
read each other's minds. They had been in agreement
about Judith's unsuitability to work for Thornton's, but
Jason Dillman had insisted it had to be her, so Natalie
had had no choice. Unfortunately it was working out as
badly as she had thought it would.

'I'll talk to her,' she sighed.

Dee raised sceptical brows. 'Will that do any good?'

'I doubt it,' she grimaced. 'But I will anyway.'

'*When* she decides to put in an appearance.'

'Yes,' Natalie gave a rueful smile, 'there is that.' In
the past Judith had only come in to see them when she
was getting short of money; the work was always
available when she wanted it, but since she had been
chosen as Thornton's Beauty Girl her appearances at
the agency had only been social ones, and not very
often.

'I know she means a lot to you, Natalie,' Dee
decided. 'But I don't think I'd be crying if she found
herself another agency.'

Again Natalie made no comment at the criticism,
knowing that it was mainly Dee who had to take the
first disgruntled calls from clients Judith had let down,
that her own calm to the stormy waters only came after
Dee had taken the worst of it.

She wouldn't be too upset if Judith left them either,
she had hoped in a way that Thornton's would take the
other girl over exclusively for an unspecified amount of
time. But the contract, drawn up by Adam Thornton's
own lawyers, demanded her services for a year only,
and at the end of that year she was free to work for
whoever she wanted to. Natalie knew she would come
back to her for work, that things were made easy for
her there. Not for Judith the effort of a taxing career—
work when you have to and play when you don't, that

was her motto—and one she lived by regardless of other people's feelings. It wasn't an easy situation for any of them.

Natalie glanced at the plain white-gold watch on her slender wrist. A white-gold bracelet on her other wrist was her only other jewellery, her fingers were completely bare of rings, the nails painted the same vivid red as her lips. 'I have to go now,' she looked up. 'I have half an hour to get to Adam Thornton's office, that should give me time.'

Dee frowned. 'But it's only a few minutes away.'

She nodded. 'I know. But he was insistent that he could only spare me fifteen minutes at eleven-thirty, so I daren't be late.'

Her assistant shrugged. 'I think it will only take you ten minutes, but you go ahead.' She smiled. 'Sounds the forceful type, doesn't he?'

'At the very least,' Natalie grimaced her agreement. At twenty-five she wasn't daunted by much, having confidence in herself and her ability. But Adam Thornton had made her feel like a gauche schoolgirl.

'I wonder what he looks like,' Dee mused.

'Awful—if he's anywhere near as unpleasant as he sounds!'

'I found his voice rather sexy,' Dee grinned. 'I go for that gravelly sound, it gives an impression of power.' She grimaced. 'He's probably awful, as you said.'

Natalie laughed. 'Probably.' She sobered. 'If Judith should happen to call or come in . . .'

'I'll keep her here,' said Dee in a hard voice. 'By force, if I have to.'

Natalie knew the other woman would too, although she put the problem of seeing Judith from her mind, concentrating on what she was going to say to Adam Thornton. She had no excuse for Judith's behaviour, except perhaps that she had warned Jason Dillman at the time. Not that that was really an excuse, more a way out, and Adam Thornton didn't sound the sort of man to let anyone out of taking responsibility for their mistakes.

Her MG was parked in the car park beneath the building, and she raised a hand to the man on the gate as she drove the sports car out into the daylight.

Late autumn, the time when all the leaves had fallen from the trees, leaving them bare and grey. The sky was also cloudy and grey, the onset of winter bringing forth an icy cold wind, something Natalie didn't feel in the warmth of her car.

She drove with a natural ability, her movements in this, as in everything, graceful in the extreme. The epitome of a hard-headed businesswoman she was not, although she could stand out for what she believed along with the best of them.

The trouble was she had no idea what to prepare herself for at this meeting with Adam Thornton! He could want to talk about Beauty Girl, or he could just want to discuss something else completely. Still, she was good at her job, she had managed to convince Jason Dillman of her competence so far, so there was no reason why she shouldn't be equally convincing in front of the head of the company.

She knew little about the man himself, which meant Adam Thornton either guarded his private life with a vengeance, or else his private life was so ordinary that it wasn't worth any newspaper writing about it. Natalie decided she liked the second version best; the idea of a middle-aged man with a harassed wife and a brood of children was much less daunting than the frightening picture that had been forming in her mind.

Frightening? She had stopped being frightened of anything the day she turned seventeen and discovered that a glowing smile and shy look from deep aquamarine eyes could melt even the hardest heart, that the soft pleading of her voice could usually get her anything she wanted. Adam Thornton wouldn't know what had hit him if he proved difficult!

She parked the MG in T.C.B.A.'s private car park, admiring the silver Porsche parked next to it. Adam Thornton, the nameplate attached to the wall read. Her brows rose. Surely a middle-aged man with a harassed wife and a brood of children wouldn't drive a car like this? It looked as · if she would have to revise her thinking somewhat.

Oh, damn the man! She got out of her car, angrily slamming the door to lock it. She didn't have the time to worry about Adam Thornton, she had a lot of things that needed her urgent attention back at the office, and the sooner she got back there the better.

T.C.B.A. occupied a whole building the size of the one Natalie rented two rooms in. Most of the ground floor was taken up as a reception area, and the heels of her stylish black shoes sank into the sea-green carpet as she walked over to the desk. The girl behind the desk was glamorous enough for Natalie to be able to offer her any number of jobs right here and now. In fact the whole building seemed to be overflowing with beautiful women as she took the lift up to the executive offices, and Adam Thornton's secretary seemed to be the most beautiful.

'Can I help you?' the woman purred, her heavy make-up perfect, just the hint of a wave in her shoulder-length red hair, her eyes were a cool green. Her pale green dress moved silkily against her body as she stood up once Natalie had given her name. 'Please sit down,' she invited smoothly. 'I'll just go and tell Mr Thornton you're here.'

Natalie moved with unhurried grace to sit in one of the four black leather armchairs in the luxurious office with the huge poster-size pictures of past advertising on the walls, having no idea how long she would be kept waiting. Ten minutes later she was glad she had sat down, as the secretary was still in with Adam Thornton.

It was a full five minutes after this when she emerged, swaying over to stand in front of Natalie's chair. She was a woman of about thirty, with a cool sophistication that enabled her to look down her haughty nose at Natalie. 'Mr Thornton will see you now, Miss Faulkner,' she drawled, just as if she hadn't kept Natalie sitting here for the last fifteen minutes.

But Natalie was very aware of it, glancing at her wrist-watch. Exactly eleven-thirty! So it was to be that sort of meeting, was it.

She stood up to follow the secretary, three or four inches taller than the other woman, the heels on her shoes adding extra inches to her already five feet eight inches in height, this fact giving a boost to the confidence that had started to wane during the fifteen-minute wait.

'Miss Faulkner,' the other woman introduced with a flourish before leaving the room, closing the door softly behind her.

But introduced to whom? The office looked empty to Natalie. It was the plushest office she had ever been in, with a sitting area to the right of her, with the same deep armchairs as in the office outside, a large drinks cabinet in the same mahogany as the wide desk directly in front of her, a wide black leather armchair with its back turned towards her the only thing remotely out of place. It was smoke spiralling from the latter that told her where Adam Thornton was, although he seemed in no hurry to acknowledge the fact.

Suddenly the chair spun slowly round. 'You managed to get here this time, Miss Faulkner,' the deep, gravelly voice mocked harshly, much more effective when not muffled by a crackly telephone line. Dee would have loved it!

Effective was a good way of describing the man himself—or electric. He seemed to fill up most of the wide-backed chair, his height as he sat seeming to indicate that he was extremely tall when standing, the dark grey pin-striped suit fitting smoothly across his shoulders, wide powerful shoulders that tapered to a narrow waist, leanly masculine. But it was his face that was electric, holding her startled blue-green eyes mesmerised. Taken as a whole it was a ruggedly handsome face, dissecting each feature in turn it was the face of a man who looked caged by the bonds of civilisation, it was the face of a savage.

Eyes the blue of an ocean glittered beneath dark jutting brows, a hawklike nose, firmly compressed lips, the cheeks lean and hard, deep lines grooved beside his nose and mouth adding to what she already guessed to be late thirties, early forties, his jaw was square and commanding, the column of his throat rugged, dark hair grew over-long past the collar of the white silk shirt he wore, the grey wings of hair over his temples adding to his distinction. His hands as he leant forward to rest them on the desk in front of him were long and tapered, the fingers on his right hand loosely holding a long thin cheroot, the smoke from which was fast filling the room, the aroma not unpleasant, as wasn't the subtle smell of his aftershave.

It seemed to Natalie as if she had been looking at him for ever, and yet it had taken only a matter of seconds to notice everything about this man, all the time knowing that she was being subjected to as thorough appraisal herself, the fierce blue eyes giving away nothing of his thoughts.

Her outwardly calm demeanour gave away nothing of the inner jolt she had felt at coming face to face with such a man, although inwardly she was a conflicting mass of emotions. He had the appearance of a leashed tiger, impatient with the bonds of civilisation that meant he had to sit behind this desk, comfortable as it was, and be outwardly polite to someone like her.

But Natalie gave away none of her own feelings, the shock at his appearance, the confusion at his magnetism, meeting his gaze steadily. 'I've already apologised,' she said smoothly. 'But if you would like me to do so again . . .?' She arched dark brows over aquamarine eyes.

'That won't be necessary,' he dismissed dryly. 'I've already ascertained the fact that you were not informed of our earlier appointment.'

Natalie looked startled. 'You have?' she frowned.

He gave an inclination of his dark head, leaning back in the chair. 'You were surprised by my call, seemed unsure of the mention of our ten o'clock meeting.' He shrugged. 'You knew nothing about it, so how could you be anything else? Please, sit down, Miss Faulkner,' he invited softly.

Natalie sank gratefully into the black leather armchair facing his across the desk, crossing one leg gracefully over the other, uncomfortably aware of the expanse of slim silky leg that was exposed as Adam Thornton rose slowly to his feet, his height seeming to fill the room, well over six feet, as she had suspected, making her feel small and slightly vulnerable.

He moved to sit on the edge of the desk in front of her, his legs long and lean, his thighs powerfully muscled. His eyes narrowed as delicate colour entered her cheeks, leaning sideways to stub out the cheroot in the onyx ashtray with slow, stabbing movements. Suddenly he straightened, his expression harsh. 'We may as well get straight to the point,' he bit out, obviously intending to do so whether she wanted to or not. 'I want the Grant girl taken off the Beauty Girl contract.'

Natalie gasped with the bluntness of the statement, biting her bottom lip as she saw the gleam of satisfaction in his eyes. Damn the man, he had enjoyed disconcerting her! But he also meant what he had said; his expression was inflexible. Her head went back in challenge. 'Why?'

His brows rose, as if he weren't accustomed to being questioned about his decisions. 'Do I need a reason?' he asked coldly.

She doubted this man ever felt the need to give a *reason* for any of his actions! And yet she felt she was owed one about such an important matter, and whether Adam Thornton liked it or not, she would have one. 'I think so,' she nodded stubbornly.

He looked at her silently for several minutes. 'Okay, Miss Faulkner,' he finally shrugged. 'You can have your reason. Your Miss Judith Grant is having an affair with the head of my Advertising Department, Jason Dillman.'

The statement was delivered calmly, without emotion, and it had all the bigger impact because of that, robbing Natalie of speech. Not that she doubted the truth of what he said, she knew Judith too well for that.

'My *married* head of Advertising,' Adam Thornton added pointedly at her silence.

Natalie closed her eyes momentarily. Judith had pulled some stunts in her time, but this was definitely the worst one to date! She had known how important this Thornton contract was to Natalie, and not only did she not turn up for photographic sessions, she was having an affair with a married employee of Adam Thornton's, something he obviously frowned upon.

A mental image of Jason Dillman came to mind—tall, a very smart dresser, very good-looking in a filmstar sort of way, with blond hair and flirtatious brown eyes. He certainly didn't give the impression of being a married man; he had asked her out several times when they had first consulted together on the choosing of the Beauty Girl. His over-confident charm hadn't appealed to her in the slightest, so she had turned him down, little dreaming he had turned his attention to Judith, and with much more success by the sound of it.

But she had to at least attempt to defend the other girl. She felt a loyalty towards her, even if Judith had proved by her actions that she didn't feel the same loyalty. 'Maybe she doesn't know he's married——'

'She does.'

'She—does?' Natalie faltered reluctantly.

'Yes,' Adam Thornton confirmed grimly. 'And if you aren't careful, she's going to get your agency a reputation for more than just modelling!'

Natalie paled. 'What do you mean?' she gasped, very tense.

The blue eyes taunted as he looked down at her, his mouth twisting mockingly. 'Use your imagination, Miss Faulkner,' he drawled. 'There's a name for models who supply more than modelling.'

'How dare you!' Natalie stood up indignantly, and then wished she hadn't as she stood only inches away from Adam Thornton, dangerously close, she felt as she moved away jerkily.

'Oh, I dare,' he drawled hardly, not at all impressed by her anger. 'And I want it stopped.'

Her eyes flashed as she looked at him, hating the way he could sit there looking so calm and relaxed when he had just accused her agency, her models, of *procurement*. 'Then talk to Jason Dillman,' she snapped. 'It takes two, you know.'

'I'm well aware of the facts of life, thank you,' he snapped coldly.

She could imagine he was more than aware of them, that he familiarised himself with those facts very often. There was an air of sexuality about the man that seemed to indicate the need to indulge in a regular physical relationship. With his wife. . .? Natalie somehow doubted he was married; she had an impression of a lone wolf, who only returned to the pack out of necessity and not through choice. That impression of a savage again!

'However,' he continued curtly, 'I feel this matter is your responsibility.'

'Mine?' she protested.

'Judith Grant is your model——'

'And *you* chose her for the job!'

Once again his brows rose. 'Not me,' he shook his head, his eyes narrowed. 'Jason.'

'But he said——'

'Yes?'

'Nothing,' she snapped, flushing at his sarcasm. 'All right, Mr Thornton, I'll talk to Judith——'

'You'll do more than talk to her if you want to keep the Thornton business.' He stood up to sit back in the swivel chair. 'You either get the girl to stop this affair now, or we drop her as the Beauty Girl.'

'That would cost you a lot of money,' Natalie reasoned, knowing the launching of Beauty Girl had cost thousands.

Adam Thornton sat forward, resting his arms on the desk-top. 'I can afford it,' he said arrogantly.

'Look, what does it matter to you?' she sighed her impatience. Judith was far from the first girl to have an affair with a married man! 'So they're having an affair——'

'It *matters* to me, Miss Faulkner,' he ground out. 'And I think it should matter to you—or *do* your models offer extra services?' He looked at her with cold blue eyes.

Natalie had never felt so angry in her life, her hand itched to make contract with the hardness of his cheek, although she restrained the impulse with effort. Losing her temper with this man wasn't going to help this situation at all.

'Well?' he rasped at her silence. 'Do they?'

Natalie's mouth compressed angrily. 'I believe I require an apology for the insult you just gave to me and the women who work for me.' She refused to waver under the steely gaze he directed at her.

'Does that mean the answer is no?' he mocked.

'Yes!'

'Pity,' he drawled unrepentantly. 'I may have had a proposition—for you.'

'Mr Thornton——!'

'All right,' he put up a silencing hand. 'If your agency is as innocent as you say it is then I apologise.' He didn't look as if the word came easily to his lips. 'But that doesn't alter the fact that one of your models is conducting an affair with one of my married employees.'

At twenty-five Natalie should have been past the stage of blushing when a man made a personal remark, and yet she hadn't expected it from Adam Thornton; their conversation until that moment had been totally removed from themselves. With that one softly spoken comment he had made her totally aware of him, of the aura of sensuality that was part of the fundamental man. And after the insults he had levelled at her today she didn't like being made aware of him in this way; she considered him the enemy—and he would remain that way! Certainly the less she had to do with him the better.

She collected up her clutch-bag, straightening her shoulders. 'I've told you I'll talk to Judith,' she said stiffly as she stood up.

'And if she won't listen?'

'I'll make sure she does,' she told him with much more confidence than she felt. She was the last person Judith was likely to listen to. But she had to try!

He nodded dismissal. 'I'll leave it in your—capable hands, then.'

Natalie gave one last angry glance at the dark head bent forward as he lit another cheroot, and the man was instantly shrouded in smoke, shielding his expression.

But she was aware of him watching her as she walked to the door, and some of the tension left her once she had reached the relative peace of her car.

But not all of it! How could Judith be so stupid as to get involved with another married man? Only too easily, as she knew from past experience.

It was just after twelve when Natalie got back to the office, and none of the anger or embarrassment she had felt when Adam Thornton made his accusations had left her, although to look at her calm demeanour no one would have guessed at her seething emotions.

Dee looked up from her work as she came into the room. 'Visitor for you in your office,' she told her cheerfully.

'Judith?' she said hopefully.

'Judith,' Dee nodded with a grimace.

Natalie strode angrily into her office, closing the door behind her to confront the girl sitting in her chair behind the desk. Her sister, Judith . . .

CHAPTER TWO

NOT that the casual observer would have classed them as such; their colouring was so different, Judith being blonde where Natalie was so dark, Judith's eyes were a clear deep blue, with none of the green that made the colour of Natalie's eyes so hard to define. Their features were completely different too, although both were beautiful. Both were slender too, taking the same size in clothes, as Natalie remembered well from their childhood when her young sister had often borrowed her clothes without asking. But Judith moved with a languid grace she cultivated, while Natalie's movements more decisive, more purposeful.

The elder by three years, Natalie had always protected her young sister as much as she was able to, although she rarely received thanks for that protection; Judith's inconsideration for the agency was proof of that.

When they had both moved to London, Judith a year after Natalie, their parents had made Natalie promise to take care of the younger girl. It hadn't proved an easy task, and the two of them had only managed to share a flat for six months before Judith moved out, claiming she had no privacy. Natalie's main emotion at her sister's move had been relief, but unfortunately her parents didn't feel the same way about it.

When she had opened the agency her worried parents had begged her to take on Judith, and although she had been wary at such a choice she had to think of her mother and father fretting for them back in Devon. Her parents couldn't possibly know just how necessary that worry was where Judith was concerned; her young sister had seemed to be involved with one unsuitable man after another the last three years. Her parents would be devastated if they knew of Judith's latest involvement. Well, she would just have to put a stop to it before they found out—and before Judith ruined her. Natalie didn't delude herself for a moment. Adam Thornton meant every one of his threats to her.

Judith stood up with that languid grace she was so well known for as Judith Grant, model. For some reason her young sister hadn't felt that 'Judith Faulkner' sounded professional enough for her career, and Natalie was now glad of her sister's conceit. At least it meant Adam Thornton couldn't even guess at their relationship. How much more scathing he could have been if he had known Judith was her sister!

'Now don't frown, darling,' Judith drawled in her throaty voice, coming round the desk to sit in one of the other chairs. 'I wasn't looking through your desk, only trying out your chair to see how you manage to sit behind that desk all day.' She grimaced. 'I couldn't do it!'

Natalie moved to sit in the chair her sister had vacated, knowing that this conversation had to be carried out on a business level and not a family one. It was going to be embarrassing enough without family involvement. 'Judith, I have to talk to you——'

'Oh, not the photographic session!' her sister groaned. 'Dee had already lectured me on how irresponsible I am.'

Natalie had completely forgotten the missed photographic session of this morning, which wasn't surprising after her meeting with Adam Thornton! 'Then I won't mention it again, except to say that it shouldn't have happened. I'm running a business here, Judith, and——'

'I thought you weren't going to mention it again,' her

sister sighed wearily, obviously bored with the subject.

'All right, I won't,' she snapped. 'Let's talk about Jason Dillman instead, shall we?' She watched Judith with narrowed eyes.

If she had hoped to disconcert her sister she was out of luck. Judith looked unimpressed with the change of subject, checking the even application of her nail-gloss with an expression of boredom.

Natalie gave an angry sigh. 'Judith, are you seeing him?'

Cool blue eyes met hers steadily. 'Of course I'm seeing him, we work a lot together on Beauty Girl.'

'That isn't what I meant and you know it!' Natalie snapped in exasperation.

'Natalie, if you mean am I sleeping with the man then why don't you just come out and say it?' Judith taunted mockingly.

'Well, are you?' she demanded.

'Yes.'

'Judith, he's married!' Natalie gasped.

'So?' her sister drawled uninterestedly.

Sometimes she felt as if she didn't know Judith at all. It didn't seem to bother her sister in the least that Jason Dillman had a wife somewhere in the background.

'He isn't happy with his wife——'

'They never are,' Natalie derided, and Judith at last gave a self-conscious grimace.

'Okay, so Kenny was stringing me along,' her sister shrugged, quickly regaining her confidence. 'And he only wanted me because his wife was having a baby and couldn't sleep with him. But it's different with Jason.'

Natalie never knew how her sister could be so sophisticated in some ways and yet so gullible where men were concerned. She had become involved with Kenny Richards about a year ago, a married man who claimed his marriage was at an end, that he intended leaving his wife, when the time was right. It transpired that Kenny's wife was very pregnant at that time, and that for the moment she couldn't sleep with him because of ill health. As soon as the baby had been born and his wife was healthy again Kenny had dropped Judith as if she were red-hot.

'Is it?' Natalie said sceptically. 'Or is he just telling you that?'

'No, he isn't just telling me that!' Judith's eyes flashed deeply blue. 'He would have left Tracy years ago if he could have afforded to.'

She frowned. 'And what's that supposed to mean?'

'Putting it crudely, Natalie, it means that Tracy holds the purse strings,' her sister drawled in a bored voice. 'And the job at Thorntons isn't to be sniffed at either. It pays well, and it's a very important position. I doubt if Thornton would be too pleased if he knew about Jason and me.'

'Does he want you for himself?' It was something that had only just occurred to Natalie. She really couldn't understand Adam Thornton's interest in the affair otherwise.

'Heavens, no!' Judith gave a disparaging laugh, her beautiful face mocking. 'Adam Thornton interested in me?' she laughed again. 'He doesn't become involved with models. The latest woman in his life is a real live princess.'

'Well, she would hardly be a dead one,' Natalie mocked dryly.

'Very funny,' Judith taunted. 'I was only trying to point out that I'm not his type.' Her eyes narrowed. 'Why so interested in him, anyway? You've never spoken of him before.'

'I'd never *met* him before,' she sighed. 'He already knows about you and Jason, Judith. He wanted to see me this morning to tell me about you. He wants it to stop, and he wants *you* to stop it.' She met her sister's gaze steadily.

'Damn!' Judith muttered, standing to pace the room. 'How on earth did he find out?'

'I have no idea——'

'We've even been meeting during the day so that he shouldn't become suspicious,' Judith continued to talk to herself as if Natalie hadn't spoken.

'Jason Dillman is the reason you've been missing the photographic sessions?' Natalie gasped.

'We had to meet some time, Natalie——'

'Not in Adam Thornton's time!'

Judith's mouth twisted. 'It isn't his time he's worried about,' she scorned. 'It's his little sister.'

'Little—sister . . .?'

'Mm,' Judith nodded. 'Jason is married to Adam Thornton's baby sister.'

'And he—You and he——' Natalie broke off, too shocked to be able to talk coherently.

No wonder Adam Thornton was so angry about the affair, no wonder he wanted it stopped immediately. His own sister's husband! Goodness, he had a right to be angry. As she was, with Judith. Her sister had always been wayward, even as a child, going for what she wanted, when she wanted, with little regard for other people's feelings. But she couldn't be allowed to get away with this; this time she had gone too far. In the past Judith might have been pampered by over-indulgent parents, but here in London it was different, here Judith would be made to think of others, Tracy Dillman for one, Adam Thornton for another, and lastly her own sister. Judith had obviously not considered the reputation of the agency when she had entered into this affair.

'How could you do it, Judith?' she demanded furiously. 'Adam Thornton's own brother-in-law!'

Her sister shrugged. 'I didn't know that when I first started seeing him, but even when I did it made no difference to how I feel about him. Why should I care whose brother-in-law he is? If the little fool can't hold on to him then she should let him go, not ask her big brother to interfere——'

'You heartless little bitch!'

'Natalie!' Judith gasped, stunned by the vehemence of Natalie's words.

'Surprised, aren't you?' Natalie snapped, her eyes like a stormy wind-tossed sea. 'You thought your older sister didn't have it in her to tell you exactly what she thinks of you,' she drew in a deep ragged breath. 'Well, I do! You've done some things in your time, but this is definitely the worst. Tracy Dillman obviously loves her husband very much, *that's* why she wants to keep him. And you come along with your beauty and availability, and——'

'That's enough, Natalie!' Judith was white too now. 'I didn't come here to be insulted!'

'Then why did you come?' Natalie's hands shook as she stood up to confront her sister. 'Certainly not to work! I want this affair stopped, Judith, or you'll be taken off the Beauty Girl contract!'

Judith remained unperturbed. 'You can't do that,' she said confidently.

'Maybe *I* can't,' she ground out, more angry than she could ever remember being before, 'but Adam Thornton can. He has lawyers in his control who could make you wish you'd never heard of Jason Dillman!'

'Never!' Judith denied heatedly. 'I love him.'

As quickly as Natalie's anger had risen it now died, her protective instinct as Judith's sister now coming to the for. 'Maybe you do think you love him——'

'I don't just think it,' her sister said firmly, 'I know it.'

'But he's married, Judy——'

'Don't call me that,' Judith snapped. 'You know I don't like it. And just because Jason signed a piece of paper seven years ago it doesn't mean he's still married. People change in seven years.'

'Then why doesn't he leave his wife?'

'I told you——'

'That he'd lose his job and his wife's money,' Natalie derided. 'I wonder which he'd mind losing the most! You can't really love a man like that, Judith.'

'But I do. And I mean to have him,' said Judith with satisfaction.

'You have to stop the affair——'

'Why?'

'Because—because it's immoral, Judith!' Natalie frowned her exasperation. 'And Mum and Dad would be shocked out of their minds if they knew about it. And lastly, because Adam Thornton will ruin this agency if you don't.'

'Ah, now we're getting to it! So much for sisterly love,' Judith said scathingly. 'This agency means more to you than anything, Natalie. More than me, more than Mum and Dad, more than any man.' Her mouth twisted. 'You really should get yourself a man, Natalie—oh, not that weed Lester,' she dismissed scornfully. 'I mean a *real* man. Maybe then you'd understand how I feel about Jason.'

Natalie ignored her sister's rudeness about Lester, knowing that the dislike between the two was mutual. Lester Fulton had been taking her out for the last three months, and the first time he and Judith had met they had taken a dislike to each other, neither losing the opportunity to make digs at the other whenever they could.

But her sister's insult about her needing a man did hurt her. She knew Judith considered her to be something of a prude because she refused to discuss her relationships with men, but that didn't mean she lacked male attention. She had had plenty of men friends the last few years, and the fact that she didn't talk about them didn't mean they hadn't been deep and meaningful relationships. Deep and meaningful—! Who was she trying to delude? She had never been in love, never felt the least inclination to be—and Judith was right about something else; she had no idea how she felt about Jason Dillman, or any other man for that matter.

'I'm not giving him up, Natalie,' Judith added vehemently. 'You can do what you like, Adam Thornton can do what *he* likes, but I will not give up Jason.' She swung the door open. 'I won't, Natalie,' and she left quietly.

Natalie put a worried hand up to her temple. She knew her sister of old, and she wouldn't stop seeing Jason Dillman. What would Adam Thornton do when he found that out?

Judith had certainly landed her in a mess this time. All through their childhood she seemed to have been getting her 'vulnerable'—vulnerable to her parents, that was!—young sister out of one scrape or another. But Judith didn't want to be helped out of this one.

She had had no idea this morning when she spoke to Adam Thornton that Tracy Dillman was his sister. Heavens, he must be furious with Judith, and in the circumstances his wish to have her removed as Beauty Girl was mild compared to what he could have done. What he could still do! Judith had refused to give Jason Dillman up, and his threat to drop any contracts with the Faulkner agency was still very real.

Dee came in with the reports sorted from this morning, perching on the edge of Natalie's desk. 'She gave you a bad time, hmm?'

'Yes,' she sighed.

'How was Adam Thornton?' Dee asked interestedly.

'Arrogant,' she answered without thinking, blushing as she saw the other woman's interest deepen. 'Well, he is,' she grimaced.

'Did he match that gravelly voice?'

Did he? Oh yes, he more than matched it, that image of a middle-aged man with a brood of children was completely dismissed. 'I suppose so,' she answered nonchalantly. 'Dee, if he should happen to telephone— I'm not in.'

Dee eyed her curiously. 'Trouble?'

'Yes,' Natalie sighed without prevarication.

'Judith again?'

'How did you guess!'

'It isn't difficult.' Her friend shook her head. 'I know she's your sister, love, but is she really worth the trouble?'

'No—but my parents' peace of mind is.' She chewed on her inner lip. 'They have no idea.'

'Anything I can do?'

'I don't think so, thanks, Dee.' Natalie shook her head, knowing she had to sort this problem out herself. If she could! 'If you could just keep Adam Thornton off my back?'

'Will do.' Dee got off the desk. 'I think I'll go home for an hour now and check on my ailing hubby.' She raised her eyes heavenwards. 'He'll probably be half dead, like all men when they're ill.'

Natalie laughed, but her humour faded as soon as the other woman had left for her lunch. The day had started out so promising, she couldn't understand how it could have gone so wrong. And she still had these damned accounts to do! She took them wearily out of her desk drawer, all thoughts of her own lunch forgotten.

It was after six when she got home, and the cool calmness of her flat seemed like a sanctuary to her. It wasn't a very big flat, just one bedroom, a bathroom, large sitting area, and a spacious kitchen, but to her it now represented home, her own home where she could just be herself. She might have acted calm in front of Dee, but today had been a strain for her, no less so because of Adam Thornton's telephone call shortly after five.

'He didn't seem very pleased when I told him you weren't here,' Dee told her with a grimace.

He would be even less pleased when he had received the same answer a couple more times. He didn't come across as a patient man, more the opposite; he seemed to have a leashed power that demanded action. How long that power would remain leashed with regard to the Faulkner Modelling Agency Natalie had no idea.

But she also had no idea what she was going to do about Judith. Her sister refused to give Jason up, and she couldn't really force her to finish with the man, although her behaviour did reflect back on the agency. But until she had worked out a solution there was no point in talking to Adam Thornton.

A relaxed soak in the bath and she felt slightly better, turning her thoughts to her date with Lester this evening. The two of them had met in the lift at work, the accountancy firm Lester worked for being in the same building as Natalie's agency. Over a period of several weeks they had progressed from 'Good mornings' to actually carrying out a light conversation if they should happen to meet.

When Lester had invited her out to dinner one evening she had been undecided about accepting. After all, a casual conversation was one thing, a whole evening together had been something else. Finally she had accepted, deciding she liked him enough to spend the time with him, liking his tall, dark good looks, the warmth of his brown eyes, the way he always dressed well. The evening had been a success, and was the predecessor of many evenings spent together during the last three months.

Judith's taunting words of this morning came back to haunt her. Not that Lester wasn't a man, he could be an ardent lover when he wanted to be, but he certainly didn't light any fires within her, no man ever had.

She returned Lester's kiss warmly when he arrived shortly before eight; he was always punctual for their dates.

'You look lovely,' he smiled. 'I've booked a table for eight-fifteen,' he looked at the practical watch on his wrist. 'We'll have to leave now if we're to be on time.'

Natalie liked the way Lester was always punctual for appointments, from promised telephone calls to actual dates. It gave her a feeling of security; in fact everything about Lester made her feel secure, his almost cosetting air making her feel protected. And after being the boss all day it was nice to feel the helpless female in a reliable man's company.

Although she wasn't quite so pleased when he offered an opinion as to how she should run her business! He noticed her rather preoccupied responses to his conversation, asking her what was wrong. As soon as she mentioned Judith's name his expression darkened.

'I don't know why you bother with her,' he scowled. 'She's nothing but a worry to you.'

'She's my sister——'

'Business is business, Natalie,' he told her pompously. 'Family loyalties shouldn't enter into it.'

Judith was the only jarring note in her relationship with Lester, and usually she steered clear of talking about her sister. But she needed to talk to someone about this latest affair with Jason Dillman, and Lester was the obvious choice. After all, he was her boy-friend, they were supposed to share things, even their problems.

Lester gave a disgusted snort when she told him about the meeting with Adam Thornton and Judith's subsequent refusal to end the affair. 'Typical!' he derided. 'Well, you have your answer, Natalie, Let Thornton dismiss her,' he said callously.

She sighed, sipping the wine Lester had chosen with their meal. Lester was a connoisseur of wines, and he had chosen this one with care. For all the notice Natalie took of it it might as well have been water! How shocked Lester would be if he knew his talent had gone to waste tonight. But she had too much on her mind to worry about Lester's pride as an expert on wines.

'It isn't as simple as that,' she shook her head, and pushed her plate away, the duck and green salad not tempting her palate tonight. 'My parents are relying on me to take care of Judith.'

He grimaced, no sympathy for her in his expression. 'A husband would do that. A sister shouldn't have to. And the way your sister behaves she isn't likely to find herself a husband—only someone else's.'

Natalie knew the criticism was deserved, that so far Judith had made rather a mess of her life where men were concerned, and yet tonight Lester's criticism wrankled. She had met his parents and older brother, and she wouldn't have presumed to say a word against any of them, even if she had found his father to be henpecked, his mother totally domineering and too deeply interested in both her bachelor sons' lives.

'It's time Judith stood on her own two feet,' Lester continued, not seeming to have noticed her slight withdrawal. 'She manages to do it most of the time, and only comes running to you when she's in trouble.'

'She isn't in trouble,' Natalie sighed. 'And she didn't come to me. I told you, Adam Thornton called me.'

'Mm,' he chewed thoughtfully on his bottom lip. 'He isn't the sort of man you should cross.'

She already knew that! 'Do you know him?' she asked.

'Of him. I've read things about him from time to time in the financial paper I read. He's a real whizz-kid.'

'Hardly a kid,' she derided dryly.

'No,' Lester smiled. 'T.C.B.A. is one of the biggest cosmetic companies in the world. The man's rolling in money. It was a real feather in your cap that you managed to get some contracts with his company.'

'It wasn't a "feather in my cap" at all, Lester,' she said sharply. 'I worked hard for those contracts.' Although with hindsight she wasn't so sure she had got them through her own devices. Jason Dillman had gone through her display book before committing himself to choosing a model from her agency for Beauty Girl. At the time she had considered it normal practice—after all, he had to see what he could be getting.

But this affair with Judith put a new light on things. An agency the size of hers, exclusive as her models were, wasn't likely to attract the attention of a company the size of Thorntons. She had a terrible suspicion that Jason's attraction to Judith might have influenced the acquisition of those contracts, the ones that came after Beauty Girl anyway.

'I know,' Lester touched her hand understandingly. 'And it would be a pity to let Judith spoil it for you. She can't get involved with Adam Thornton's brother-in-law.'

'She already is!'

'Then stop her.'

'How? I've already told her about Adam Thornton's threats. She didn't seem very impressed,' Natalie derided.

'Then maybe you and Adam Thornton are going

about this from the wrong angle,' Lester frowned. 'This Jason Dillman sounds on the mercenary side, maybe he's the one you should put the pressure on?'

Why hadn't Adam Thornton thought of that? Or didn't he have that sort of influence over his brother-in-law? Of course he did. And it was up to him to stop the affair if she couldn't. She certainly wasn't going to worry about it any more, and she smiled brightly at Lester as she changed the subject. She could deal with the problem of Adam Thornton tomorrow.

She encouraged Lester to talk about his work, marvelling at his ability to deal with the sort of figures that had become her nightmare.

'Maybe you should become my accountant,' she teased him.

'I don't think you could afford my prices,' he answered her seriously. 'Do you really enjoy running the agency, Natalie?' he frowned. 'It seems to me to be nothing but trouble.'

'I enjoy it,' she said stiffly. 'It's my independence.'

Lester moved closer to her on the sofa, the two of them having returned to Natalie's flat a few minutes earlier, lingering over their late-night coffee. 'Maybe I would rather you weren't so independent?' he murmured softly. 'Perhaps I'd like you to cling a little more.'

Natalie gave a nervous laugh, not liking his serious air. 'Don't you like career women?' she teased.

'Not much,' he answered bluntly.

'Lester!' She moved back to look at him in stunned surprise.

'Well, I don't,' he shrugged. 'When I marry I want my wife to concentrate on being my wife and the mother of my children.'

That sounded exactly like his mother! 'Wouldn't that be a little boring—for your wife?' she mocked, having visions of herself as another Mrs Fulton. Oh dear, no!

He looked affronted. 'I don't think so—Why are you laughing?' he frowned at her humour.

Because if she didn't laugh she would cry! This conversation had become too serious for her liking—she had no doubt that Lester saw *her* as the 'little woman' who would stay at home and look after him and the children. She was fond of him, but the thought of being the sort of wife he wanted filled her with horror.

'I'm only teasing you, Lester,' she smiled. 'I'm sure the woman you choose to be your wife will be happy to take care of you and your children.' But it certainly wouldn't be her!

'You think so?'

'I'm sure of it,' she said briskly, standing up to put an end to the evening. 'It's getting late, Lester . . .' she told him pointedly.

'Oh yes.' He accepted her words at face value, having no idea of the almost-panic he had caused within her. He put the empty coffee cup down on the table in front of him, and stood up to face her. 'Lunch tomorrow?'

'Fine,' she agreed brightly, knowing she would have to end this relationship slowly if she wasn't to appear too obvious in her fright.

He bent to kiss her softly on the mouth. 'Twelve-thirty?'

'Lovely,' she nodded, edging him towards the door.

He left a few minutes later—much to her relief. What a day it had been! That awful meeting with Adam Thornton, her sister's stubbornness, and now she had found out that the current man in her life was secretly a male chauvinist.

And tomorrow didn't promise to be any better!

Surprisingly her morning passed quietly enough. She had appointments with a couple of clients, ones she had a feeling she was desperately going to need if she lost the Thornton contracts.

She heard nothing from Adam Thornton, and she was loath to call the man herself. If he had already spoken to Jason Dillman and the other man had refused to end the affair, as Judith had, then he could put the ball back in her court. Ignorance was bliss in this case. At least it was peaceful!

A red-faced Dee came into her office shortly after eleven. 'I don't think he's going to be put off much longer, Natalie,' she said worriedly.

'Hm?' Natalie looked up vaguely.

'Adam Thornton, he——'

'Has he been calling?' Her eyes widened, deeply aquamarine.

'All morning,' Dee nodded. 'At least, his secretary has. I managed to put her off, but this last time he called himself. I don't think he believed me when I said you weren't in.'

Natalie frowned. 'But I—Damn, I forgot to tell you I'd take his call,' she groaned, cursing herself for her stupidity. She had completely forgotten to tell Dee to divert his calls.

'You mean I've been putting him off all morning and your really wanted to talk to him?' Dee grimaced.

'Sorry,' she said ruefully. 'Has he telephoned a lot?' She sat back, her make-up as perfect as always, her hair a gleaming ebony bob, the turquoise of her silky dress seeming to match the colour of her eyes.

'Half a dozen times at least,' Dee moaned. 'And this last time he sounded furious!'

Natalie gave a worried sigh. 'You'd better call him straight back. I'm really sorry about this.'

'Don't be silly,' her friend dismissed. 'You have a lot on your mind.'

Even more so now! 'That may be so, but I don't

have to be stupid with it,' she derided. 'How's Tom today?'

'The same,' Dee grimaced. 'Men!'

It was a statement Natalie heartily echoed. Men! And one man in particular.

Dee buzzed through on the intercom a few minutes later. 'He isn't there,' she told Natalie ruefully.

'Really? Or is his secretary just saying that?' It would be just like Adam Thornton to decide not to talk to her now that she had called him.

'Well, she said he wasn't in the office before I told her who I was,' Dee explained. 'So I would say he really isn't there. Do you want me to keep trying?'

'Please.'

A glance at her wrist-watch told her it was almost eleven-thirty. Maybe he had gone to an early lunch. He was probably tired of having to trouble himself with such a nonentity as Natalie Faulkner. She doubted if he usually bothered himself with such things, and wouldn't have become involved this time if it weren't for his sister's happiness.

She had no warning as five minutes later Adam Thornton strolled forcefully into her office, no knock, no call from Dee, just the arrogantly overpowering man suddenly standing in front of her desk.

She had forgotten how tall he was, how dominating. The whole room seemed to be filled by him, and his savagery was even more apparent today, his expression impatient as he looked down at her with steely blue eyes.

Natalie noticed everything about him in that shocked first few seconds—the cut of the navy blue three-piece suit he wore with the pale blue shirt, the rugged handsomeness of his face, the distinctive grey hair at his temples, the black sheen to the rest of his thick over-long hair. Yes, he was everything she remembered—and more.

'I'm sorry, Natalie,' a flustered Dee had followed him. 'He just walked in.'

Natalie was aware of the arrogant challenge in steely blue eyes as she tried to look at Dee. 'It's all right,' she soothed. 'This is Mr Thornton—Mr Adam Thornton,' she added pointedly, her mouth twisting at the awed Oh! Dee gave.

He turned to look at the other woman. 'And you're the competent young lady who's been baulking my secretary all morning,' he drawled huskily. 'I could use someone like you in my own office,' he smiled.

Natalie gave a dazed blink as she too was caught up in the charm of that smile, mentally shaking herself to break the spell he was casting. Just because the man looked ten years younger when he smiled, the grooves in his cheeks deepening, the sudden warmth of blue eyes, it was no reason to feel any less nervous of him. This man was dangerous, ruthless, and she would have to remember that.

'Thank you, Dee,' she dismissed the other woman, seeing her friend's grimace of disappointment before she went into the outer office, closing the door behind her. 'Now, Mr Thornton,' she looked up at him coolly. 'What can I do for you?'

He pulled up a chair, lounging back against the white leather, taking his time in answering as he lit one of the cheroots he favoured, having the look of a slumbering black leopard about to spring.

Finally he looked up, his eyes narrowed against the smoke. 'Well, you can call me Adam for a start,' he drawled softly. 'I have a feeling we're going to be working closely together in future, close enough for you to call me Adam, anyway.' He looked at her challengingly.

Natalie eyed him warily. 'What do you mean?'

'It's quite simple,' he mocked. 'I've decided to

personally handle any work connected with this company. I would also like to accept any of the fringe benefits *you* might be inclined to offer with those contracts.'

CHAPTER THREE

NATALIE gasped her outrage; she had never been so insulted in her life before. 'I run a business here, Mr Thornton,' she snapped angrily. 'A legitimate business!'

'I'm sure you do,' he seemed unimpressed. 'But I'm also sure you must realise that my company doesn't usually do business with an agency as small as this one?'

Her eyes glittered dangerously, her hands tightly gripping the edge of her desk. 'Are you implying that I told Judith to sleep with your advertising manager just so that we would get the Beauty Girl contract?' Her voice was soft, furiously so.

Adam Thornton shrugged, perfectly relaxed, blowing smoke-rings up at the ceiling. 'No, I'm not implying that——'

'Good!' she bit out.

'But I am *saying* that this agency got that contract because Jason had already slept with this girl Grant.' He watched Natalie with narrowed eyes.

She flushed, uncertainty flickering in her eyes. 'Could you explain that remark?' she requested coolly.

'It's quite simple,' he drawled. 'Jason knew this girl Grant before he came to your agency. The two of them met at a party months ago. They were lovers before he even approached you about Beauty Girl.'

'Oh no!' she groaned, feeling sick, but knowing it was the truth. It would explain so much.

'Oh yes,' Adam Thornton confirmed dryly. 'Needless to say, I knew nothing about it.'

'Neither did I,' Natalie snapped challengingly.

'Didn't you think it rather strange that a company the size of Thornton's should come to you?' he derided scathingly.

'And didn't you think it strange that Jason should use an agency of this size?'

He shrugged. 'One thing Jason has always been is good at his job. He claimed the Grant girl was the most suitable, so I went along with that.'

'And I've built up quite a good reputation this last year,' she defended heatedly. 'It was conceivable that we'd been recommended to Mr Dillman from another company.'

'Conceivable,' he nodded. 'But not very likely. Or were you just so surprised at your good fortune that you didn't like to question it too deeply?' The blue eyes were icily contemptuous.

Natalie knew there was a certain amount of truth in what he said, that she really hadn't been able to believe her luck. But at the time it had been exactly the boost her agency needed, getting them noticed by other companies at the same time.

She looked at Adam Thornton, wishing he didn't look quite so self-confident, that he didn't *know* he was right. But she doubted this man was ever wrong! 'I'm sure you'll agree,' she said stiffly, 'that the work my models have done for you has been as professional as any of the other agencies you deal with.'

'Except for the Grant girl,' he nodded. 'And we all know the reason she's inefficient.' He viciously stubbed out the cheroot.

'Do we?'

'She's too damned busy spending her mornings and afternoons in bed with Jason!' he rasped.

Natalie paled, swallowing hard. 'You—you mean you know about that?'

'I've made it my business, now, to know about the

whole affair,' he ground out savagely. 'I also know that Jason refuses to end it. Did you have any better luck than I did?' he questioned sharply.

She chewed on her bottom lip. 'Er—no,' she admitted.

His mouth compressed angrily. 'Is that why you've been avoiding my calls?'

Wild colour flooded her cheeks, highlighting the strange blue-green of her eyes. 'That was a mistake——'

'I agree, it was,' he drawled mockingly. 'You wouldn't have had to confront me in person if you'd taken my call.'

'That wasn't what I meant,' Natalie snapped agitatedly. 'I—I told Dee I wasn't taking any calls this morning—I didn't think about your calls at the time,' she invented. 'As soon as I realised what had happened I had Dee call you back. You'd already left to come here,' she finished reluctantly, knowing that he *would* have been less forceful down a telephone line.

His mouth twisted mockingly. 'I'm not used to being fobbed off in that way.' He stood up, at once seeming to fill the whole room again, the movement made with the languid grace of a jungle cat. He glanced at his wrist-watch, a plain gold affair that had probably cost a year of Natalie's salary. 'Ten past twelve,' he murmured thoughtfully. 'Get your coat, Natalie, we're going to lunch.'

She looked up at him open-mouthed, as much for the fact that he knew her first name as for what he had said. Still, it wasn't so surprising when looked at logically; he had probably found out all that he could about the Faulkner Agency when he had realised what was happening between his brother-in-law and one of their models. He probably knew everything about her, right down to her bra size! No, she looked at him thoughtfully, he looked as if he had enough experience to be able to guess that without help from anyone.

She blushed as he raised his brows enquiringly. 'I don't go to lunch until twelve-thirty today,' she told him haughtily, knowing she still had those bright wings of colour in her cheeks.

'Are you the boss?'

'Yes,' she frowned.

'Then you go to lunch at what time *you* want to. Get your coat,' he repeated abruptly.

Natalie looked at him with rebellious eyes. 'Maybe I just don't want to have lunch with you, Mr Thornton.'

Amusement lightened his eyes. 'I'm sure you don't,' he derided. 'But get your coat anyway.'

'I——'

'This is business, Natalie,' he rasped. 'You surely didn't think I was about to demand those "fringe benefits" right now?' he taunted softly.

She drew in an angry breath. 'There are no fringe benefits!'

'No?'

'No!'

Adam Thornton pursed his lips thoughtfully. 'Then maybe I should just try and think of a few I might like from you.' There was a warmth in his eyes now, where before there had only been condemning coldness.

Natalie couldn't believe this was happening. Adam Thornton was actually flirting with her! 'You can think in vain, Mr Thornton,' she said stiffly. 'All you'll get from this agency—from me,' she added pointedly, 'is efficiency.'

'It will do for the moment,' he shrugged. 'Now, are you going to keep me waiting much longer for my lunch? I should warn you,' he taunted, 'I get even more unbearable when I'm hungry.'

Her mouth twitched as she held back her humour. 'Who was brave enough to tell you that?'

Adam Thornton felt no such reluctance, and smiled openly, instantly looking younger once again. 'A young lady who knows I love her too much to be angry with her.' His expression had softened indulgently.

Natalie looked away. 'I see,' she said quietly.

'My sister,' he mocked.

She chewed her bottom lip. Her own sister's behaviour seemed all the more terrible now because of this man's undoubted love and concern for his sister. God, she was feeling guilty now, and it was none of her doing!

'What is it?' Adam frowned.

'Nothing,' she dismissed firmly. 'Lunch is really business?'

'Of course,' he derided. 'Although I hope you'll forgive me if I enjoy the food.'

She ignored the sarcasm. 'You would like to leave now?'

'If not sooner,' he nodded.

Natalie smiled mischievously, unable to resist it. 'You do get grouchy, don't you?'

'Very,' he confirmed abruptly. 'But I've also been assured that I'm a pussycat when I've eaten.'

Her mouth quirked as she tidied her desk in preparation for leaving. 'Your sister again?'

'Mm.' He took her black velvet jacket from its hanger behind the door and held it out to her.

Natalie slipped her arms inside the jacket, moving swiftly away from the warmth of his body, aware of the tangy smell of his aftershave, the pleasant smell of the cheroots that clung to his clothing.

She ignored him as she retouched her lip-gloss, very selfconscious as she knew he watched her in the mirror, his enigmatic blue gaze fixed on her parted lips as she applied the plum-coloured gloss.

'Don't you know,' he murmured as she turned, his

body suddenly close against hers, 'that watching a woman do that only tempts a man to taste those lips for himself?' His voice was softly seductive.

Natalie swallowed hard, suddenly finding herself dangerously close to him, and lost her balance slightly as his arms moved confidently about her, putting a steadying hand on his chest, feeling the rapid beat of his heart beneath her palm as she looked up at him with dazed eyes. She was tall herself, but Adam Thornton was at least six inches taller as he towered over her.

She felt mesmerised by intense blue eyes as his head slowly lowered and his mouth claimed hers. No exploratory kiss this—his lips instantly parted hers, moving druggingly against her, forceful against her mouth as she would have refused his access.

She couldn't refuse this man anything; she could feel herself melting against the hardness of his body as he pulled her between his parted legs, his hands moving restlessly across her back, seeming to burn her flesh through her dress, one hand moving to her nape as she would have drawn away from him.

He took his fill of her, tasting her mouth in slow drugging movements, his breathing ragged and his eyes glittering with desire when he at last released her mouth to look down at her. 'You taste—delightful,' he told her huskily.

Natalie pulled out of his arms, straightening her dress selfconsciously. Yesterday she had decided that the man wasn't alive who could light a fire within her, and all the time it had been Adam Thornton, her adversary, the most mocking, arrogant man she had ever met.

And yet her pulses still leapt, her body still trembled, her mouth still throbbed from his touch. At this moment she could have forgotten everything but being in his arms, knowing the pleasure of his mouth once again.

'But I know by the taste of your lips that you aren't wearing a Thornton lip-gloss,' he added derisively, breaking the mood.

She gave him an irritated glare, wanting to hit out at him for causing this confusion within her. 'I don't happen to like their shades.'

His brows rose. 'What's wrong with them?'

Maybe she wouldn't have been quite so outspoken if she hadn't wondered just how many women he had kissed to be able to tell one of his own products just by the taste! It somehow seemed to throw her own fiery reaction to his kiss out of all perspective. She was twenty-five years old, not a naïve schoolgirl to be impressed by the experience of an older man, an arrogant overbearing man at that.

She shrugged, shaking her head. 'They do nothing for me.'

He moved impatiently to the door, not liking the criticism. 'I suggest you retouch the lip-gloss—a second time, while I tell your secretary you'll be out to lunch.'

Natalie reapplied the lip-gloss without really thinking about it, glad of this respite to collect her scattered thoughts together. So the man knew how to kiss—so what? So she had responded like never before. She had been taken by surprise, it certainly wouldn't happen again!

'What about Lester?' Dee asked when Natalie joined them in the outer office a few minutes later, perfectly composed now—on the outside, at least. 'Shall I call him and tell him you can't make lunch?'

'Oh—yes.' She avoided looking at Adam Thornton after his first speculative glance. 'If you wouldn't mind,' she nodded. 'Explain that it's business, will you,' she added to let Adam Thornton know that as far as she was concerned that was *exactly* what it was. 'I'll call him this afternoon.'

'Fine.' Dee seemed perfectly willing to accept this, now that she knew this man was Adam Thornton. 'See you later,' she added lightheartedly.

'You may do,' Adam Thornton drawled, taking a firm hold of Natalie's arm.

She allowed him to guide her out to the lift, standing silently beside him as they went down to the ground floor, stepping into the back of the burgundy-coloured Rolls-Royce as the chauffeur held the door open for her and Adam Thornton climbed in beside her, nodding coolly to the straight-faced man. Somehow Natalie had been expecting the silver Porsche, and the Rolls came as something of a surprise to her.

'Who is Lester?' Adam asked softly as the chauffeur smoothly drove the car out into the traffic, a glass partition between the back and the front of the car closed for greater privacy.

Natalie turned to look at him, slightly overwhelmed by the obvious wealth of this man. 'He's—a friend,' she answered, wary of his interest.

'I see.'

She frowned. What did he 'see'? She had no idea, because he made no further attempt at conversation until they were seated in the restaurant, the famous Savoy Grill Room. Natalie had been here with Jason Dillman during business meetings, and remained unimpressed today because of that, ordering only a green salad and steak for herself, but not in the least surprised when Adam Thornton ordered a four-course meal for himself.

'What business did you want to talk to me about?' She looked at him coolly, firmly putting that kiss to the back of her mind—as he seemed to have done.

Adam sipped his whisky, perfectly relaxed, taking his time about answering her. 'A Fantasy Girl,' he finally answered her.

Natalie's eyes widened. 'Fantasy Girl . . .?'

He nodded. 'I may have given you the wrong impression of my opinion of your work on Beauty Girl——'

'I don't think so,' she snapped.

'I think I did,' he smiled, sitting back as their meal arrived. 'Judith Grant may have been chosen for all the wrong reasons, but I can't deny her success. That line is turning out to be one of our most successful. It was a very good idea to take a complete unknown and make her Beauty Girl.'

'Then Jason Dillman hasn't done everything wrong,' Natalie taunted.

'I hate to disappoint you,' he mocked, 'but the unknown was originally my idea; Jason merely followed it through. You may remember that we also had a new perfume out at about the same time; I was concentrating more fully on that.'

She nodded. 'You used two of my models.'

'So we did,' he acknowledged. 'Also hand-picked by Jason.' He sighed. 'I begin to suspect those two as well.'

'You needn't,' she bridled. 'Gemma and Sheri are both happily married.'

'That's a relief,' he frowned.

'Fantasy Girl . . .?' she prompted, very interested in what sounded like yet another new project. T.C.B.A. were really expanding at the moment—and she would like to be in on that.

'A new line of make-up with a more defined shading, deeper, but also brighter,' he explained.

Natalie nodded. 'Just right for today's fashions.'

'Exactly,' he agreed. 'Maybe even you'll wear it,' he added mockingly. 'I'd like you to find my Fantasy Girl for me. Not literally, of course,' he derided.

'Of course,' she said stiffly.

'Do you think you can do it?'

'I think so, yes,' she answered slowly. 'Although I shall need to know a lot more about the make-up.'

'Naturally. Although I hope it's understood that what I've so far told you about Fantasy Girl is not for public knowledge.'

Natalie stiffened. 'I'm not completely stupid, Mr Thornton!'

'You aren't stupid at all,' he rasped. 'That's part of the reason I'd like to work with you on this.'

'With you . . .?' Her appetite had suddenly deserted her.

Adam raised dark brows. 'Do you have any objections to working with me?' he challenged.

Did she? The less she had to do with this man the better, from a personal basis, but as far as the agency was concerned it could be the making of them. Beauty Girl being one of her models was one thing, but with a follow-up . . .! The agency, and she, would never look back.

'You seem undecided,' Adam Thornton drawled. 'Believe me, Natalie, if I'd known that the Ms Faulkner who ran the agency was such a beautiful woman I would have ousted Jason before now.' The blue eyes openly caressed her. 'Why are you behind the desk and not out there in front of the cameras?' he demanded suddenly.

She remained cool in the force of his flattery, wanting to remind him that this was a business meeting—even if it was the most unusual one she had ever had! 'I was in front of the cameras for a while,' she shrugged. 'It isn't enough for me.'

'No,' he mused, 'I don't suppose it is.'

She eyed him suspiciously. 'Why don't you?'

His brows rose. 'Do you always bristle this easily?'

'Always!'

'Should be fun,' he mocked.

'What should?' Her voice was sharp.

'Working with you.' He sat forward, his hand covering hers. 'I believe I shall enjoy it very much.'

Natalie could feel herself blushing. 'What will happen about—about Beauty Girl?'

His face became harsh, and he removed his hand from hers. 'I've tried to reason with Jason, you've tried to reason with Judith Grant—I may just have to drop her,' he said curtly.

'No! I mean—Couldn't you give it a little more time?' She blushed at his narrow-eyed look, aware that she sounded as if she were pleading with him, feeling angry with Judith for putting her in such a position with this man. 'Maybe the affair will just—die out, of its own accord,' she added hopefully.

He shook his head. 'In my estimation it's gone on for almost nine months already,' he ground out.

Natalie chewed on her top lip, feeling dismayed at her sister's stupidity. 'Does—does his wife know?'

'No!' he rasped. 'And I don't intend that she should.'

'I—I had no idea she was your sister,' she said apologetically, feeling a guilt herself.

'I don't make a habit of admitting to Jason being my brother-in-law,' he dismissed harshly.

Natalie looked down at her hands. 'Do they have any children?'

'No, thank God!' His savagery was back with a vengeance, as he signalled to the waiter to bring their bill. 'Judith Grant is only the last in a long line of women who flit in and out of Jason's life. Tracy seems to love him so much that it never occurs to her that he has affairs,' Adam ground out. 'If it wasn't for Tracy's love I would have thrashed hell out of the bastard before now!'

She could see that. And he would extract extreme pleasure from doing so.

'As it is,' he continued, scowling, 'I shield her from his behaviour as much as possible. It isn't always easy. And as for his job as my advertising manager—all his work will be done behind a desk in future,' he stated in a flat voice.

Natalie was surprised that Jason Dillman dared defy this man, although the leverage of his young sister's happiness was enough to keep Adam Thornton's actions to a minimum. She was ashamed that her own sister should be involved in this sordid affair. If Adam Thornton should find out that Judith was her sister . . . Heavens, she would hate all of his savage anger to be turned on her! And if Judith had any sense she would be wary of him too. But her sister had always lived by the dictates of her heart and not her head.

Adam Thornton's chauffeur drove them back to her office, where Adam got out of the car with her, although he didn't go up to the office with her. 'Think about the new contract,' he encouraged huskily. 'I'll be in touch.'

'Er—when?' Natalie delayed him getting back into the car.

He turned back to her, his harsh mouth twisted into a smile. 'It will be soon,' he said gruffly, his hands coming up to frame her face. 'Very soon,' his lips briefly claimed hers. 'Are you seeing your friend Lester this evening?' he asked softly.

She was very conscious of the stone-faced chauffeur standing beside the open back door of the car, her embarrassed gaze flickering over him and then back to Adam. 'Yes,' she answered shakily, knowing she couldn't become involved with this man.

'Pity.' He released her abruptly. 'I'll call you, Natalie. And this time I think you should be in.'

She stiffened at his warning tone. 'I'll try,' she told him coolly.

He smiled, a hard, humourless smile. 'You'll do more than try.' He nodded abruptly before climbing back into the car, not looking at her again.

Natalie turned to make her way slowly up to her office. Through lunch she had managed to convince herself she had imagined that instantaneous and fiery reaction to Adam Thornton's kisses, but this last brief time in his arms had convinced her that she hadn't imagined anything. She didn't even like the man, even if she could respect him as a businessman, and the way she had responded to him frightened her a little. Adam Thornton was a man to beware of, for more reasons than one.

'I've been married three years, and he had the same effect on me!' Dee teased.

She looked up, her smile rueful as she realised she had been so deep in thought she had been going to walk straight into her office without even saying hello. 'Sorry,' she grimaced. 'And he is a little—overwhelming.'

'A little?' Dee raised her eyes to the ceiling. 'He's beautiful. I wonder what he looks like without his clothes?' she mused.

'Dee!'

'I know, I know,' the other woman smiled. 'We women aren't supposed to think of such things. But we do, don't we?'

'I——'

'Don't we, Natalie?' Dee's mouth quirked with humour.

Delicate colour ebbed into Natalie's cheeks at the thought of that virilely handsome man naked beside her. Dee was only putting into words what she had been imagining, nevertheless she still found it embarrassing to realise she had had such thoughts—and about a man she hardly knew. She had been seeing Lester for months, and not once had she had such thoughts about him.

'You may as well go to lunch now, Dee.' She didn't answer the other woman. 'And give Tom my love.'

'I will.' Dee stood up. 'Maybe you can give Mr Thornton mine the next time you see him,' she added mischievously.

'I have no idea when that will be,' Natalie returned stiffly. 'Did you talk to Lester for me?' she changed the subject.

Dee nodded. 'He said not to telephone this afternoon because he won't be in the office, that he'll call for you at eight-thirty.'

'Thanks.' Natalie bit back her irritation, and went through to her own office to deal with the calls that had come in for her while she had been out. She hadn't wanted to see Lester tonight, in fact after their conversation last night when she had realised he had her in mind for the possible role of a loving housewife and mother she wasn't sure she wanted to see him again. She had enjoyed being with him, but marriage was definitely out. Her mother might consider that at twenty-five she was on the shelf, but as far as she was concerned she had plenty of time yet to get married and settle down to wedded bliss! It had taken her long enough to get the agency established, she certainly wasn't going to give it up now, and certainly not for Lester. She liked him, but she couldn't love him.

The agency, and she, were on their way to the top if Adam Thornton chose his Fantasy Girl from one of her models. If, that was the question. If Judith ruined this with her stupid affair with Jason Dillman she would—would what? Judith was her sister, and family loyalty had to count for more than the agency.

Lester was his usual thoughtful self that evening, and

yet Natalie parried his unusually passionate goodnight kiss with a light laugh.

'I missed you at lunch today,' he groaned against her throat. 'I had something important I wanted to discuss with you.'

Natalie stiffened, moving easily out of his arms, standing up, very beautiful in the lamplight, her green dress clinging to her. 'I have something I want to tell you about too.'

'You do?' His expression brightened; his jacket was discarded, his shirt partly unbuttoned down his chest.

The two of them had been out to dinner, and had returned to Natalie's flat for coffee. They had finished drinking the coffee ten minutes ago, and now she wanted to avoid any possibility of personal conversation between them. She intended finishing this her own way, the way she usually did, by always being too busy to see Lester when he called. After a couple of weeks of this avoidance he would realise she had no intention of seeing him ever again. Cowardly, but effective.

'I saw Adam Thornton again today.' She spoke of the first thing that came into her mind, and then wished she hadn't. Adam Thornton was a subject she wanted to avoid.

Lester looked irritated by the mention of him too, obviously wanting to talk about something else entirely, like their future together.

Natalie shuddered. 'He's pleased with the work we've done so far,' she told Lester brightly. 'He's even hinted that he might give us another important contract.'

'Very nice,' Lester said uninterestedly. 'Natalie, I really——'

'Don't you think it's wonderful?' she continued determinedly. 'I can hardly believe my luck!'

'Yes. But, Natalie——'

'I have such a busy day tomorrow, Lester,' she

feigned a yawn, 'I really must get some rest now.'

'But——'

'Please, Lester,' she smiled at him sleepily. 'We can talk another time.'

He stood up to impatiently pull on his jacket, not pleased with the abrupt end she was giving the evening, but too polite to push the matter. 'Tomorrow at lunch,' he told her firmly.

'Er—not tomorrow.' She edged him towards the door. 'I'll have a lot to do the next few days. I'll call you when I'm free, shall I?'

'But——'

'Yes, I'll call you, Lester.' She held the door open pointedly.

'Very well,' he snapped, kissing her briefly on the mouth. 'But I really do have to talk to you, Natalie.'

'Of course.' She smiled at him brightly as she stood in the doorway while he stepped into the lift, going back inside her flat as soon as the lift doors had closed.

She sank down wearily in a chair, ashamed of the way she had opted out of telling Lester she didn't want to see him again. Judith would certainly never have hesitated.

Judith. She knew she would have to talk to her sister again about Jason Dillman. And she wasn't looking forward to the conversation.

Contacting her sister was something else completely. Judith didn't appear to be at her flat the next morning, and as she didn't come into the office Natalie knew she would have to leave it until tonight when, she hoped, Judith would have returned home.

In the meantime she had other models to deal with, other clients, and her morning was kept fully occupied. There was no call from Adam Thornton, and she knew he was going to make her wait on his decision concerning Fantasy Girl. But she would be prepared for him when he did contact her; she already had three of her models in mind. Fantasy Girl should be someone dramatic, the epitome of every man and woman's fantasy, a woman that men ached to take to bed, a woman other women longed to look like. Most men were supposed to prefer blondes, and yet Natalie knew that it was usually blondes that other women tended to be wary of—a fallacy, but she believed it to be very widely accepted as fact. Therefore, Fantasy Girl should be dark, beautifully, exotically dark, with the sort of complexion that should take the dramatic make-up T.C.B.A. were aiming for. Three of her girls could fit that description, and she had prepared a file on them for when Adam Thornton did contact her. When . . .

Once again she had no warning of his arrival. The door suddenly slammed open, and if anything Adam Thornton looked even more angry than he had yesterday. What had she done this time?

Dee gave a worried grimace behind his back, as she pulled the door closed. Adam's anger seemed to fill the room.

Natalie looked up at him nervously, totally intimidated, wondering when he was going to speak. He seemed too angry to be able to say anything, the fierceness of his expression silencing her own words in her throat.

Suddenly he moved, coming round the desk to pull her roughly to her feet, his fingers biting into her arms through the white and candy-pink striped dress she wore, a dangerous glitter to his narrowed blue eyes, his mouth twisting savagely before it ground down on hers.

He was intent on inflicting pain, and he was succeeding. Her whimpers sounded low in her throat as he ruthlessly crushed her against his hard body, bending her to his will.

Just when she thought she would break in two he released her, so suddenly that she fell back against the desk, bruising her thigh. But that was nothing to the painful throb of her lips, and the inside of her mouth felt ragged and sore as she raised her fingers to it.

'Now that I've got that out of the way,' he ground harshly, 'maybe you wouldn't mind telling me why you didn't inform me of the fact that Judith Grant is your sister?'

CHAPTER FOUR

'I——' NATALIE faltered.

'Well?' he barked.

Her eyes flashed at his impatience. 'If you'll just give me chance——'

'To do what?' he demanded, towering over her ominously, the dark brown suit and cream shirt he wore emphasising the darkness of his skin. 'To think of an excuse as to why your own sister was chosen as Beauty Girl? To think of a reason you kept quiet about that little fact even though you knew the cold-hearted little bitch could ruin my sister's life?'

'No!' She had gone very white.

'No?' he bit out disbelievingly.

'Once and for all—no!' she glared at him furiously. 'You know as well as I do why Judith was chosen.' She wet her lips nervously. 'Explaining why I didn't tell you she's my sister could be a little harder.'

'I'm sure it could!' he glowered.

'But you're coming here and—and manhandling me,' she said agitatedly, 'has certainly done nothing to help the situation.'

'It was either beat you or kiss you—I preferred the latter,' he told her grimly.

'There was no reason for either——'

'No?' he mocked harshly. 'I've just had a very unsatisfactory meeting with your sister.'

'Judith . . .?' Natalie swallowed hard.

'Yes,' he snapped. 'And may I say that I hope to heaven you have none of your sister's nature. So far I can see no similarity, and I hope there isn't any.'

She could see his disgust for her sister clearly revealed in the depths of those fierce blue eyes, the hard lines of his face appearing as if carved from granite. 'I—what did she have to say?' she asked hesitantly.

'The—details of it need not concern you,' he told her coldly. 'Your sister has six months of her contract with us left to run, at the end of that time she'll be dropped from our advertising campaign for Beauty Girl.'

It was no worse than she had expected, in fact it was better. She had thought Judith would be dropped instantly, in fact Adam Thornton had threatened as much. What had happened to change his mind? 'And—er—Fantasy Girl?' She looked at him as if waiting for the axe to fall.

And fall it did. Adam Thornton looked down his arrogant nose at her. 'I've decided to go elsewhere for my Fantasy Girl,' he stated coldly. 'To a more—respectable and trustworthy agency.'

'Oh, but——'

'I trust I make myself clear, Miss Faulkner?' he added haughtily.

She hated the way he raised his eyebrows so condescendingly, and a flush coloured her cheeks. 'Very,' she mumbled.

'Good,' he said with hard satisfaction, straightening his cuff. 'Goodbye, Miss Faulkner.'

'Er—goodbye,' she echoed dejectedly, suddenly finding herself alone once more.

So much for her hopes and dreams of yesterday! Adam Thornton was more than angry now, he was thoroughly disgusted. And there was no way she could redeem herself, or her agency. She would have to wait and see if he would influence any of her other clients away from her, something he was perfectly within his rights to do. Judith's behaviour had been unethical, to say the least.

'Bad news?' Dee had come in without Natalie being aware of it.

She grimaced, not wanting to show the seriousness of what had just happened, but in reality she felt like crying. 'Well, it wasn't good,' she said lightly.

'I thought he was going to beat you when he stormed in here!'

Dark colour flooded her cheeks as she recalled the punishment he had extracted instead of the beating, her lips still feeling swollen. She put her hand up to them selfconsciously, sure that she had no lip-gloss left. 'He isn't that uncivilised, Dee,' she said awkwardly, knowing just how close she had come to that beating.

'He comes over as very uncivilised to me,' Dee murmured dreamily. 'Sort of rugged and untamed. He would have made a good caveman!'

'Too intelligent,' Natalie said without thinking, surprised at the other woman also noticing that air about Adam Thornton, and flushing as she saw Dee's speculative look. 'Well, he is,' she insisted. 'If he had been a caveman he would certainly have been head man!'

'Undoubtedly,' her friend nodded. 'I can just see him hitting the woman of his choice over the head and dragging her off by her hair to his cave! The thought gives me goose-bumps!' She gave a pleasurable shiver.

Natalie raised mocking brows. 'How is Tom today?' she enquired dryly.

'He's fine, back at work—thank goodness! And there's no harm in a little daydreaming,' Dee grinned. 'I'm too much in love with Tom to do more than that. It's a pity you got off to such a bad start with him,' she grimaced.

'Yes,' Natalie sighed. 'Er—no,' she denied once she had realised what she had admitted to. But she couldn't help wondering what sort of effect she and Adam

Thornton would have had on each other if they had met in different circumstances. 'Not my type at all, Dee,' she said briskly, evading the other woman's probing glance as she moved to sit behind her desk.

'Why?'

'I—Well—Too bossy,' she dismissed.

Dee's smile deepened. 'I would doubt he needs to be bossy with women very often!'

So did Natalie. Dee wasn't impressed very easily by men, her attitude towards them was slightly cynical, something Natalie usually found amusing. They had both agreed that Jason Dillman was a shallow flirt, and now they both agreed that Adam Thornton was the opposite, that the man probably had depths no one was allowed to probe.

But she didn't want to think of Adam Thornton any more, she had more pressing matters on her mind. 'Could you try Judith's flat again?' she requested briskly. 'And if she isn't there just keep trying until she is. I want to see her immediately,' she added hardly.

'Okay. I——'

The outer office door slammed, and a flushed and angry Judith marched into the room. 'Arrogant bastard!' she snapped furiously, throwing herself down into a chair to glare up at them, her expression one of rebellion.

Dee gave Natalie a rueful shrug. 'I'll talk to you later. Good morning, Judith,' she mocked.

' 'Morning,' Judith muttered as the other woman left the room, looking more beautiful than ever in her anger.

'And who is the arrogant bastard?' Natalie enquired softly, sure she already knew who it was.

'Adam Thornton,' her sister confirmed, her blue eyes blazing, her mouth set angrily.

'Why?' she probed softly, sure she would get more

out of Judith than Adam Thornton had been willing
to reveal.

'He had the nerve to tell me I have to give up Jason!'

'Yes?'

'He even threatened me when I refused!' Judith
sounded almost surprised.

Natalie didn't find her sister's surprise in the least
puzzling. Ever since they were children Judith, as the
younger, had been cossetted and cared for, never denied
even her smallest wish, and Natalie knew that she had
been as guilty of the spoiling as her parents had been;
all of them had loved her too much for her own good.
Judith simply didn't understand why anyone should
deny her anything, not even someone else's husband.

'How did he threaten you?' she prompted quietly.

'He told me he was sacking me as Beauty Girl!'
Judith revealed indignantly.

Natalie stiffened, knowing that Adam hadn't carried
out that threat. Why hadn't he?

'I soon told him,' Judith added with satisfaction.
'He's so set on protecting his sister that when I
threatened to go to her and tell her about Jason and me
he backed down.'

Heavens, her sister was so stupid! Men like Adam
Thornton didn't 'back down'. He was simply biding his
time, and when he was ready, probably at the end of
Judith's contract with him, he would strike. He would
probably make sure she never got another modelling
job in her life.

She sighed her exasperation. 'Only until your
contract with him runs out——'

'By that time it won't matter,' Judith dismissed
confidently. 'Jason will have left his wife by then.'

'To do what?'

'Marry me, of course,' her sister derided.

'And what will he do for a job?'

'He's always wanted to set up his own advertising agency. In America. Where Adam Thornton can't touch him.'

Natalie held back her own anger with difficulty, knowing that there wasn't a place where Adam Thornton 'couldn't touch him'. 'Would he take you with him?' she asked drily.

'Of course.'

'And what do you think that will do to Mum and Dad?' she snapped.

Judith looked disconcerted for a moment, but only for a moment, her confidence returning with a dismissive shrug. 'I'm sure they'll love Jason.'

'They may do,' her parents would like anyone if Judith claimed them as a friend, 'but I doubt they'll love the fact that he's married.'

'He'll get a divorce——'

'Which will take years!' Her anger got the better of her now. 'You're completely irresponsible, Judith—selfish, thoughtless, and irresponsible.'

'And you're just jealous!' Her sister stood up. 'Because Jason wants me and not you.'

'I——'

'I won't listen to you any more,' Judith told her furiously. 'I intend to continue seeing Jason, no matter what anyone says—or does!'

'Even if you hurt people in the process?' Natalie almost shouted.

'It would hurt *me* too much to give him up!'

The two of them continued to glare at each other, then Judith suddenly turned on her heel and left, leaving the smell of her heady perfume behind her.

Natalie sat in stunned silence, more sure than ever now that she didn't really know her sister any more. They had come a long way from the time they had lived in Devon with their parents, sharing a bedroom, sharing secrets of current boy-friends as they talked long into the night. She could no longer reach her sister, not even the disillusioned hurt of their parents could do that now.

How could Judith have threatened to tell Tracy Dillman about her affair with her husband? And how dared she make that threat to Adam Thornton? Judith might not realise it, but the payment for that threat had already started, in Adam Thornton's withdrawal for a Fantasy Girl. How much more vengeful he would be when Judith's contract ran out!

It was Natalie's turn to telephone her parents that weekend, and in the circumstances she wished she didn't have to. They were sure to ask how Judith was, and with the disgust she felt towards her sister she didn't think she could answer them rationally.

'Your mother is just having a lie-down,' her father told her. 'She's feeling a little tired now that the season is over.'

Her parents ran a small hotel on the sea-front in the Devonshire town they had lived in for the last thirty years, despite the fact that her mother had suffered from high blood pressure for the last ten years.

Natalie frowned, knowing how rarely her mother admitted to the weakness of being tired, seeing the chance to be able to discuss her worries over Judith fast disappearing. Her father already had enough to worry about.

'We didn't hear from Judith last weekend,' her father added almost wistfully.

'She's very busy with Beauty Girl at the moment,' she answered vaguely, angry that her sister had missed her turn to telephone their parents. She knew how they worried about their daughters.

'We've seen her photographs in the newspapers, and

she was even on television the other day,' their father said proudly.

'Yes,' Natalie said dully.

'It's so nice to know that we have no worries with our two girls,' he added confidently.

No worries! Judith was conducting an affair with a married man, was also ruining Natalie's agency in the process. No worries?

'Natalie?' Her father sounded concerned at her silence.

Her reply was bright and reassuring. 'No, we're both doing very well.'

'Good. And don't mention your mother's tiredness to Judith, it would only upset her.'

With the wholly selfish attitude she had discovered in her sister lately Natalie wasn't so sure it would worry Judith at all. Although perhaps she was being unfair, Judith had always been close to their mother, just as she had always been closer to her father. How she wished she could unburden her troubles to him now!

But she couldn't, and wouldn't, not even mentioning the mess Judith was making of her life. Surely at twenty-two Judith was old enough to control and decide her own life. If only she hadn't decided on a married man, a married man who could cause nothing but trouble!

Lester called her towards the end of the following week, and out of desperation she accepted his invitation to the theatre, then wished she hadn't, as it turned out to be one of those plays she detested, a handful of actors debating on the reason for mankind.

She had agreed to the date out of a need to take her mind off her other problems, and at the end of the first act she was so bored with the play that her mind kept wandering to her problems anyway. Despite what her

father had said about Judith not being told of their
mother's tiredness she had casually mentioned it to her
sister. Judith's answer had been that she would go home
'some time' to see their parents. As it was almost a
month since she had last been home Natalie wondered
when 'some time' would be.

'Natalie!'

She blinked up at Lester as he stood in the aisle next
to her. 'Hmm?'

'I said would you like to go for a drink during the
interval?' he repeated impatiently.

'Yes, please.' She followed him out to the bar, glad of
a reason to stop thinking.

'I'll just go and get our drinks,' Lester told her once
they had reached the crush of people in the lounge area,
the people about the bar seeming to be about four deep.
'You wait here.'

Gladly. She had no wish to get caught up in that
crowd. But the time alone gave her even more time to
think. It had been a terrible week so far, and she still
had Friday to go! As she had suspected, Adam
Thornton hadn't stopped with the dropping of Fantasy
Girl, she had received several cancellations this week
from clients she had received through the promotion of
Beauty Girl, and several of her other long-standing
clients were suddenly unavailable when she telephoned
them. She had no doubt that Adam Thornton was
behind it, she knew what a powerful man he was in the
world of business.

She felt a little conspicuous standing here alone in the
crowd, almost as if she were being observed. She slowly
looked about the room, her eyes widening as she saw
Adam Thornton standing a short distance away, a
beautiful redhead clinging to his arm, her figure and
features almost doll-like. But Natalie spared only a
glance for his beautiful companion, finding fierce blue

eyes watching her intently, making her very conscious
of her own appearance, although she had no need to be.
The black and grey dress she wore fitted perfectly, the
grey evening bag and matching high-heeled sandals
complementing the outfit. She looked cool and
attractive, although the white-gold bracelet she wore,
her only jewellery, couldn't hope to compare with the
emerald and diamond necklace and bracelet the other
woman wore.

Her heart leapt in her throat as Adam Thornton
turned to say something to his companion before
coming towards her, carrying his glass of whisky with
him. Of course he would have a drink, Natalie thought
bitchily, no queueing up at the bar for him!

'Miss Faulkner.' He stood in front of her now.

'Mr Thornton.' She met his gaze unflinchingly.

'Enjoying the play?' he drawled pleasantly, almost as
if he hadn't threatened her the last time they had met.

'Yes, thank—No,' she admitted ruefully.

'Terrible, isn't it?' he surprised her by agreeing.

'Yes. But if you don't like it——'

'Unfortunatley my companion is a patron of the
arts,' he gave rueful sigh. 'She helped finance this play.'

Natalie looked past him to the tiny but beautiful
woman, the dark green dress she wore of the finest silk.
'The princess?' she guessed, remembering what Judith
had said about this man's latest woman-friend.

'Who told—Your sister,' he derided. 'Yes, Maria is a
princess—an Italian princess.'

Her eyes widened. 'I didn't know there were any.'

'Oh yes,' he sounded amused. 'Although she rarely
uses the title.'

'It could come in useful when booking into a hotel or
restaurant,' Natalie smiled.

'No doubt,' he nodded, not returning the smile. 'I've
been meaning to call you, Miss Faulkner.'

She instantly stiffened. 'You have?' Her tone was instantly apprehensive, forcing a smile to her lips as Lester turned and caught her eye, at the bar now, waiting for their drinks to be served. He frowned slightly as he saw Adam Thornton standing at her side, turning away as the barman demanded his attention.

'Lester?' Adam Thornton asked softly, having followed her line of vision.

'Er—yes,' Natalie confirmed awkwardly. 'What were you going to call me about, Mr Thornton?'

He shrugged, looking magnificent in the dark evening suit, the grey hair at his temples giving him a very distinguished look. 'I hardly think this is the place for a business talk,' he drawled mockingly as the crowds of people jostled noisily about them. 'Perhaps you could call me in the morning?'

She swallowed hard. 'If that's what you would prefer,' she nodded.

'I would. Now if you'll excuse me . . .?' he said distantly, not sparing her another glance, striding back to Princess Maria's side, receiving a pouting look for his absence, though the pout disappeared as his mouth briefly captured the bright red lips.

Natalie turned away, uncomfortable at watching such an act of intimacy. Fortunately Lester was pushing his way back to her side, and by the time she had thanked him for the drink and taken her first sip Adam Thornton and the Princess had disappeared.

'Who was that man?' Lester frowned.

'Adam Thornton.' She didn't prevaricate, she was too deeply disturbed by the telephone call she had to make tomorrow morning. What could Adam Thornton want to talk to her about? Had Judith been up to something else? But he hadn't seemed angry or annoyed, in fact he had been quite pleasant. Too pleasant . . .? After the way they had last parted maybe he had been. Now she was really worried.

'Did he say anything about the other contract?' Lester asked vaguely, intent on finishing his drink before they had to go back into the theatre for the second act.

'No,' she answered, relieved when the interval bell rang.

She couldn't help it, as soon as they were once more seated she began to look around the theatre for Adam Thornton. It didn't take her long to spot him; he and the Princess were sitting in the principal box. Steel blue eyes looked down on her mockingly, and she quickly looked away again. Damn him! What *did* he want to talk to her about?

She asked herself the same question many times during the sleepless night she spent, the last of many just lately, and she got into the office a little after eight. She busied herself with her work until the clock slowly crept round to nine o'clock, nine-fifteen, nine-thirty. Surely she could call him now without appearing too eager? She thought she could.

Dee got back to her within minutes. 'He isn't available at the moment, Natalie,' she said regretfully. 'Shall I try again in a few minutes?'

Natalie chewed agitatedly on her bottom lip. 'Yes, try again soon.' She waited impatiently for the next hour, finally buzzing back through to Dee. 'Did you——'

'I've called him twice more, Natalie,' the other woman assured her. 'He isn't available.'

Damn him, he was doing this on purpose, the way that she had done to him. He certainly liked exacting the maximum of revenge! 'Call him once more, Dee,' she said determinedly. 'And if he still isn't available tell his secretary I'll be in to see him at eleven-thirty.'

'But——'

'Tell her, Dee,' she said firmly.

A few minutes later Dee actually came through to her office. 'He still wasn't available,' she told her ruefully. 'So I passed on your message.'

'And?' Natalie's fingers tightly gripped the pen she was holding.

'And his secretary said that he had another appointment then——'

'I don't care if he has fifty appointments!' Her eyes glittered fiercely blue-green. 'I intend seeing him today. Call her back, Dee, and——'

'But he can see you at twelve-fifteen instead,' Dee finished pointedly.

'Oh,' she blushed.

'All right?' Dee asked gently.

'Fine,' she nodded ruefully.

'That's what I told her,' her friend nodded. 'Anything I can do, Natalie?' she asked concernedly.

'Nothing at all.' Natalie shook her head. 'I think this is something Adam Thornton and I have to work out between us.'

'Good luck!'

She had a feeling she was going to need it, although she looked cool enough in front of Adam Thornton's sophisticated secretary when she arrived at his office at exactly twelve-fifteen—she wasn't going to be kept waiting this time!

This time she felt calm enough to notice the other girl's nameplate on the front of the desk: Cara Shaw. She also noticed the most recent framed poster of the Thornton beauty advertisements, one of Judith as Beauty Girl. Oh, how Adam Thornton must be regretting that!

'Mr Thornton will see you now,' Cara Shaw told her huskily.

None of her nervousness showed as she walked into the

executive office, as she squarely met the cool blue gaze blatantly searching her pale cheeks, slowly moving down to her pert breasts, narrow waist and slender thighs, making her feel naked, despite knowing the rust-coloured blouse and black suit gave her a businesslike appearance.

'Come in and sit down, Natalie,' Adam invited softly, bending forward to light one of his cheroots, slipping the gold lighter into the pocket of the grey waistcoat that matched the rest of his suit.

So it was 'Natalie' today, she noticed, feeling a little like a fly invited in by the spider as she closed the door and moved to sit in the chair opposite him.

'Well?' he asked after several silent seconds.

She blinked dazedly. 'Yes?'

'You said you wanted to see me—or rather, your secretary did,' he taunted.

'I—No—I——' He had deliberately put her at this disadvantage, damn him! '*You* were the one who wanted to talk to me,' she told him determinedly.

He shook his head slowly. 'I asked you to call me.'

'And I did,' she said impatiently. 'Several times. You weren't available.'

'Really?'

She glared at him, sensing his ridicule, although his expression was innocent of mockery. Too innocent. 'Really!' she ground out, feeling even more like that fated fly.

'I had a board meeting this morning,' he dismissed.

'I see,' she said tightly. 'Then why couldn't your secretary have just told me that?'

Adam raised dark brows. 'I never reveal my actions to people over the telephone,' he drawled. 'And I'm not going to make you the exception to that rule.'

His insulting tone was barely disguised, and Natalie flushed uncomfortably. 'I'm sure you aren't. Now could we get to the reason you wanted to talk to me?'

'If you insist,' he nodded. 'It's about my sister——'

'I've already told you I can't do anything about that affair, Mr Thornton,' she sighed impatiently.

'I believe I said *my* sister, Natalie,' he said, dangerously soft.

She flushed at the rebuke, her hands clasped in her lap. 'Yes?' She looked at him resentfully.

Adam Thornton leant back in his chair, smoke surrounding him like a cloak. 'Did you enjoy the play last night?'

Natalie frowned her consternation. 'You know I didn't,' she snapped impatiently, knowing he had watched as she and Lester left before the end of the play—as had a lot of people. She had been aware of those ever-watchful blue eyes following her progress out of the theatre. 'Your sister——'

'Maria has atrocious taste in plays,' he mused softly, ignoring her mention of his sister. 'Fortunately her other—tastes aren't quite so misguided,' he drawled.

Natalie gave an impatient sigh, not missing the innuendo. 'Your sister, Mr Thornton,' she reminded him hardly, not liking this cat-and-mouse game at all.

'Yes,' his steely eyes suddenly looked straight into hers, 'my sister,' he nodded. 'I believe you've been having some difficulty at your agency the last few days?' he raised dark brows.

She frowned. 'Yes . . .'

'I'm sure you're aware of the reason for that difficulty?' he continued in that infuriatingly polite voice.

'Yes,' she acknowledged, very tense now.

'I believe I may have found a way to allay this— difficulty.'

She swallowed hard, eyeing him suspiciously. 'How?'

Adam smiled, the slow taunting smile of the victor.

She doubted this man was ever anything else! 'I want your help.'

'My—help?' she repeated incredulous, sure there was no way she could possibly help such a man. Unless——

'No,' he drawled mockingly, 'I don't need to use such devious means to get a woman into bed with me.'

'No—I'm sure you don't,' she said awkwardly, wondering what had happened to the confidence she had had about this man before she had met him, the way she had been sure she could handle him with her usual smile and clear blue-green eyes. She never knew where she was with this man! 'Then what can I do to help you?' she enquired coolly.

'Does that mean you would have no objections to—helping me in that way?' he taunted.

'Mr Thornton!' she gasped her indignation.

'All right,' he sat forward, all amusement gone, 'I want your help for Tracy.'

Natalie couldn't conceal her puzzlement. 'How could I help your sister?'

'Quite easily.' He stood up. 'If your regret about your sister's affair with Jason is sincere.'

'It is!' her eyes flashed.

Adam looked down at her for long timeless minutes, the blue eyes seeming to see into her very soul. 'I believe you,' he said finally, heavily.

'Thank you!'

The blue eyes became frosty, his mouth thinned. 'I find this distasteful enough, without your damned sarcasm!' he snapped, his anger threatening to boil over and shoot Natalie up in flames with him.

'I'm sorry——'

'I doubt it,' he bit out. 'But you will be if my sister doesn't take to you. I want you to become her friend, Natalie,' he explained at her gasp of surprise. 'I want you to show her that there's more to life than Jason Dillman.'

'But——'

'Tracy married Jason when she was only eighteen—against my wishes, I might add,' he said grimly, staring out of the window, but seeing nothing, his thoughts all inwards. 'But she was of age, there was nothing I could do to stop her marrying him. Once it became fact I tried to help them; I only gave Jason the job at Thornton's because of Tracy. Although there's no doubting his ability to do the job, not even for Tracy could I allow an idiot to be in charge of my advertising.'

'Of course not.'

His eyes narrowed at her sarcasm, but he didn't reprimand her for it. 'They'd only been married a few months when I discovered that Jason was conducting an affair with a girl who worked for him in advertising. I managed to stop the affair before Tracy found out. The next time I wasn't so lucky.' His mouth was set grimly. 'Tracy was almost hysterical when she realised what was happening. I wanted her to leave him, to come home, but the little fool——' he took a deep controlling breath. 'She forgave him after he swore it would never happen again. As far as Tracy is concerned it never has.'

Natalie felt deeply for his young sister, for the love she felt for the faithless Jason. 'And in reality?' she prompted huskily.

Adam's hands clenched into fists. 'He's been continually unfaithful to her—affairs I've kept from her, I'm ashamed to say,' he said bitterly.

'How can I help?'

'Do you want to?' He looked at her searchingly.

'I think so,' she nodded.

He sighed. 'Tracy is beautiful,' he told her without conceit. 'Sweetly beautiful. And intelligent. But she's known no other life than being Jason's wife since she was eighteen years old, and it suits Jason to keep her that way. It doesn't suit me,' he ground out. 'Maybe if she comes out into the real world, if she's forced to, she'll see Jason for what he is—or at least have the sophistication to hold and keep him.'

Natalie frowned. 'Why don't you just tell her?'

'And lose her love?' he said in a pained voice. 'Tracy is the one person I love in this life——'

'As I love my sister!'

'Yes,' he rasped, 'I'm sure you do. But she's going to be hurt too in the end.'

'I know,' she sighed.

'Jason has used the knowledge of my love to maintain my silence over the years, knows I would never do anything that would cause Tracy pain.' He shook his head. 'I don't intend it to remain that way any longer.'

'What are you going to do?' Natalie frowned.

'Me? Nothing.' Adam sighed his impatience with the love that held him silent.

Her eyes widened. 'You surely don't expect me——'

'No,' he dismissed mockingly. 'All I want from you is friendship for her. You have a successful career, and that career gives you independence. I want Tracy to see that she can have those things too, either as Jason's wife—or not,' he finished simply.

It didn't seem so much to ask, and considering the part her sister was playing in all this it wasn't much at all. 'Judith believes Jason is going to leave your sister soon anyway,' she told him absently.

His mouth twisted derisively. 'Then she's as much of a fool as Tracy is. If there's ever an end to their marriage Tracy will have to be the one to make it. Jason's too secure the way he is to rock the boat.'

That was what Natalie had thought, what she had tried to convey to Judith. But, as Tracy had, her wilful, headstrong sister would have to find that out the painful way.

'Will you do it?' Adam was watching her closely. 'Just be her friend, show her what she could have?'

'Are you sure I'm the right person to ask?' She hesitated about committing herself. 'After all, Judith is my sister.'

'And, as I've already pointed out, you're not at all alike,' he said harshly. 'I've had you, and your agency, checked out, Natalie,' he told her arrogantly. 'You have a good reputation, both in business and as a person. In fact,' he added softly, 'you're exactly the sort of person Thornton's like to do business with. I believe I mentioned Fantasy Girl to you . . .?'

'Are you trying to blackmail me, Mr Thornton?' she bristled.

'Let's just say I'm offering you an incentive. Business is full of such incentives nowadays,' he taunted. 'You might even find that all those people who have suddenly been unavailable to you will suddenly be just as available.'

Angry colour heightened her cheeks, and she stood up angrily. 'I think you'd do better to ask your—friend the Princess for help. I really don't think I can be of any assistance to you.'

He met her gaze mockingly. 'I want a woman who's a success. Maria's only business interest is in the theatre—and you saw how successful she is at that! Besides which, Tracy isn't very fond of her. No,' he drawled, 'it has to be you or no one, Natalie.'

'And if I refuse?'

He shrugged. 'I believe you already know the answer to that.'

Natalie was shaking with anger, could have hit him and not felt an instant of regret—except that he looked the sort to hit her back! 'So I have no choice?' she said stiffly.

'None.'

'And if your plan fails?'

'I try never to think in terms of failure,' he told her haughtily. 'You would do well to do the same.'

'All right,' she sighed her capitulation, knowing she really hadn't had a choice from the beginning, 'I'll do it.'

Not by the flicker of an eyelid did he show he was pleased by her answer, merely nodding, as if her answer had been a foregone conclusion. 'I'll make the arrangements for the two of you to meet,' he said briskly, once more the controlled businessman. 'You'll like Tracy,' he added confidently.

Which meant she had better!

CHAPTER FIVE

NATALIE was in a constant state of tension the next week, expecting to hear from Adam Thornton at any time about the proposed meeting with his sister.

He didn't call, but he had been right about her other clients, most of them called *her* to make appointments, and these appointments kept her very busy.

But not too busy to think of Adam Thornton. She had committed herself to seeing a lot more of him, of becoming involved with his family too. And Judith still refused to give a damn!

She called round to Natalie's flat one evening during the week. 'Jason has to accompany Tracy to her aunt's for dinner,' she explained her free evening, 'so I thought I'd come and see you.'

'Thanks!'

'You aren't going out, are you?' Judith lounged in one of the armchairs, her denims and tee-shirt skin-tight.

'No,' Natalie answered dryly, having had her solitary dinner and intending to have a quiet evening reading the paperback she had bought at the weekend. Judith looked in a chatty mood, so the paperback would probably go unread for another evening.

'No Lester?' her sister taunted.

'No,' she said tautly. 'And I don't enjoy being visited because you're at a loose end.'

Judith looked bored by the reprimand, ceasing to take notice of Natalie's disapproval years ago. 'I called Mum last night.'

'Yes?'

'She does sound tired, as you said,' she frowned. 'I've told them I'll go down at the weekend.'

'I'm sure they were pleased,' Natalie said without rancour, accepting after all these years that her sister, as the baby of the family, had a special place in their parents' affections.

'Mm,' Judith grimaced. 'I shall be bored out of my mind,' she drawled. 'But at least I won't have to go again for a few months. Jason's going to be busy over the weekend anyway.'

Natalie gave an impatient sigh at her sister's selfishness. 'Don't you ever get sick of sharing him, Judith?'

She looked surprised by the question. 'I don't share him,' she snapped. 'He's already mine. It's only a matter of time.'

'That's what I mean.' Natalie stood up impatiently, very slender in black denims and a red blouse. 'If he's really serious about you, Judith, why hasn't he left his wife?'

'I told you, he's——'

'Going to,' Natalie nodded. 'Why the delay, Judith? Why not leave her now?'

Her sister shrugged. 'Because the time isn't right yet.'

'For whom?'

Judith moved uncomfortably. 'If you're going to be unpleasant——'

'I'm trying to act as a sister should,' Natalie interrupted softly. 'To point out the mistake you're making. I'm sure that if Jason were really serious about you he would have left his wife by now, no matter what the cost to him personally.'

'All well lost for love, and all that rubbish?' Judith taunted.

Natalie blushed at her sister's derision, often feeling as if she were the younger of the two. Judith certainly had more experience than she did! 'Something like that,' she mumbled.

'Real life isn't like that, Natalie,' Judith mocked. 'Jason has to wait until the right time, until he has everything arranged for the two of us to go to America with the minimum of fuss. Besides, I have this damned Beauty Girl contract to finish yet.'

'You didn't feel that way about it at the start,' Natalie said dryly.

'No,' her sister shrugged. 'But that was because I wasn't so sure of Jason then.'

'And you are now?'

'Yes!' Judith sighed her impatience. 'For God's sake stop nagging, Natalie. It isn't going to change a thing, no matter what you say.'

No, she could see that. Judith had to run the course of this affair, as she had with Kenny Richards, even if she became more badly hurt than before. 'All I ask is that you don't tell Mum and Dad about him yet,' she pleaded softly. 'They wouldn't understand.'

'They have to know some time——'

'But not yet,' she said firmly. 'Please, Judith.'

For a moment her sister looked rebellious, then she capitulated. 'All right,' she agreed moodily. 'I feel like being spoilt this weekend anyway.'

And they both knew she wouldn't be if their parents were told, that they would be bewildered and hurt, and that they wouldn't understand.

As Natalie didn't! She might have experienced a few moments of mindless pleasure in Adam Thornton's arms, but she still had no idea how Judith could feel so strongly about a man that she thought him worth destroying her whole life for, especially as that man was Jason Dillman.

Judith's visit had been two days ago, and it was Thursday now, and she still hadn't heard from Adam

Thornton about her meeting with his sister. She had considered telephoning him, but finally convinced herself that in the circumstances no news was good news.

She had a dread of Tracy Dillman liking her no better than she did the Princess. Because if she didn't this whole thing was going to cave in about her ears.

When the doorbell rang on Thursday evening, interrupting the reading of her paperback, she felt only trepidation as to who was on the other side of the door. She didn't want to see either Judith or Lester, and she knew it couldn't be anyone else.

Her eyes widened when she opened the door to Adam Thornton, an Adam Thornton she barely recognised, the black denims fitting tautly across his thighs and legs, the black silk shirt fitted to the powerful breadth of his chest, his hands thrust into the pockets of a tan leather bomber jacket.

The blue eyes were mocking as her startled gaze clashed with his. 'May I come in?' he drawled.

'Of course,' Natalie answered confidently, conscious of his gaze burning into her back as she led the way into the lounge, looking around the room anxiously, relieved to see that it was as neat and tidy as usual, bright and welcoming too. She had nothing to be ashamed of about her home, although she felt sure this man usually surrounded himself with more luxury than she could afford.

She did, however, wish she could have been more smartly dressed herself; her denims were old and faded, very tight-fitting, the masculine red and black checked shirt tucked in neatly at her waist, dramatically unbuttoned to the curve of her breasts. It was the latter she was selfconscious of, her naked breasts firm and uptilting against the cotton material, obviously so. But she hadn't been expecting company tonight, so she had dressed for comfort and not style; her face was bare of make-up too.

Adam Thornton seemed to find nothing wrong with her appearance, in fact his gaze was warm as he slowly looked her over from her head to her bare feet.

Natalie moved the latter selfconsciously, feeling about ten years old. 'Has anything happened?' she frowned.

'Not that I know of,' he dismissed casually. 'May I sit down?'

'I'm sorry——' She touched her lips with the tip of her tongue, turning away as she saw those intense blue eyes following the movement. 'I'm being a very bad hostess,' she said in a flustered voice. 'Please sit down. Can I get you a drink?'

'Whisky?' Adam lowered his lean length into an armchair, stretching his long legs out in front of him, looking perfectly relaxed, an impression that was belied by the aura of leashed power that surrounded him.

'Of course,' she nodded. 'Ice, water, a mixer?'

'Straight.'

Of course! She could only drink the strong alcohol when it had been liberally mixed with lemonade, but this man would drink his whisky neat, and he wouldn't even flinch as the fiery liquid passed down his throat.

Natalie's thoughts were chaotic as she moved about her kitchen pouring his whisky, and a Martini and lemonade for herself—she might need it! Why was Adam Thornton here? What was he going to say to her?

He was still relaxed in the chair when she rejoined him, taking his drink, his fingers brushing against hers, his brows instantly raised as she hastily moved away.

Natalie sat opposite him, her legs curled up beneath her in the chair, her bare feet hidden from his narrow-eyed gaze. It was strangely silent—and electric, sitting here in the intimacy of her flat with this man, knowing he had been the one man to break through her coolness, to light a fire within her. She was terrified of that fire, frightened that if he touched her again she would go up in flames. It wasn't a pleasant feeling, not when he was also her enemy.

'Do I make you nervous, Natalie?' he softly interrupted her tortuous thoughts.

She blinked rapidly. 'Why should you think that?'

He shrugged. 'Just an impression I have.'

'The right impression,' she admitted softly. 'Do I have to remind you that you threatened me the last time we spoke?'

'Not threatened, Natalie,' he denied. 'I had the leverage to obtain your help for my sister, so I used that leverage. But your agency will benefit too.'

'Yes,' she acknowledged huskily.

'I came here tonight to tell you what arrangements I've made.'

She was suddenly wary. 'Yes?'

'Yes,' his mouth quirked as he picked up her mood. 'You're invited to dinner on Saturday—at my apartment.'

Natalie stiffened, her eyes wide. 'I couldn't——'

'Jason and Tracy have been invited too,' he added mockingly, sipping his whisky.

'Oh.' So that was the reason Jason was going to be 'busy' this weekend!

'Disappointed?' Adam taunted.

'No, of course not,' but to her chagrin she blushed, something she seemed to do all the time about this man, something she didn't usually do at *any time*.

Blue eyes seemed to see into the depths of her very soul, darkening in colour at her confusion. Adam moved slowly to his feet, putting his glass down on the table, moving to stand in front of her, his legs braced apart as he put out a hand to pull her to her feet. 'I am,' he murmured, inches taller than her now that she was in her bare feet, 'very disappointed.'

'Adam . . .!'

'Natalie,' he taunted, his hands firm on her spine as he pulled her into him, the heat from his body engulfing her. 'Do you have any idea how damned beautiful you are?' he rasped.

'Adam!' she gasped again at his aggressive tone.

'Too damned beautiful for my peace of mind!' he bit out, his head bending as his mouth laid claim to hers.

The embers of desire ignited to a flame, and with a soft groan of capitulation her arms went up about his neck, straining against him as she met the passion of his mouth. His hands ran urgently over her body, arousing where they touched, fingers exploring the hollows of her throat, daring the open neckline of her shirt, moving beneath the material to capture one aching breast, caressing the sensitive nipple with unerring accuracy.

Her sigh of pleasure was lost against his lips, allowing her to show her desire for him as his thighs surged throbbingly against hers, causing pleasure and pain at one and the same time.

The buttons of her shirt were deftly dealt with, the over-large article of clothing caressing her heated flesh as it was slowly pushed from her body, then Adam captured her breasts with surprisingly gentle hands, touching the sensitive tips with caresses that made Natalie feel weak with longing.

It was only two steps to the sofa, and the material felt cool against her bare back as Adam bore her back against the cushions, his dark head bent to her breasts in reverent adoration.

Natalie's head went back at the first touch of his moist tongue on the hardened nipples, warm pleasure invading her body as he sucked the sensitive tip into his mouth, pleasuring with his lips, teeth, and tongue, to cause a frenzy of emotions to hurtle through to the very tips of her toes.

His jacket was discarded now, his shirt quickly following, his skin moist and salty as she rained fevered kisses over his naked torso, feeling the ripple of muscle in his back as her hands clung to him there.

She felt no embarrassment, only pleasure, as her denims and panties were expertly removed, leaving her naked beneath him, the warm throb of his body crushing her into the sofa as he lay on top of her, the heat of his lips against her moist flesh sending rivulets of pleasure down her spine.

'Adam!' she gasped as her passion rose. 'Adam! Oh ... !' She felt lost, totally in Adam's control, having no will of her own—and not wanting one. She desperately needed to know what was at the end of this wild spiral of desire, to know the full sensation of Adam's pleasuring.

'It's all right, darling,' he soothed, kissing the moist fullness of her mouth, easing the tension she felt, gently reducing her passion until she lay quivering in his arms, the bewilderment in her eyes silently reproaching him. 'Now isn't the time for us, Natalie.' He gently caressed the side of her face, smoothing the damp hair back from her forehead, kissing her brow, cradling her against him as they lay side by side on the sofa, his other hand curved about her hip as he held her to him.

Her breathing was ragged as she felt passion ebb, although the sensuous feel of his naked chest beneath her cheek held desire on the very edge of cascading into a vortex of mindless pleasure.

'That's it, darling,' he said throatily, his hands shaking slightly. 'Cling on to me. You understand why I had to stop when I did?' His dark blue gaze burnt into hers as he looked down at her flushed face.

Her hand rested lightly on his chest, the world slowly

swinging back on its axis, her confusion all the deeper as she became aware of her nakedness. How could he stop, how could *any* man stop, when he had already been so deeply committed to making love to her, when she lay here naked against him?

'Don't look at me like that, Natalie,' he groaned. 'It isn't easy for me either.'

'Then why——'

'Because when I make love to you I want to give you all my attention, show you all the consideration a beautiful woman like you should have. If I start an affair with you now I'll forget about everything else, including the mess my sister has made of her life.' He shook his head. 'I can't let it go on for her like this any longer. You do understand, Natalie?'

She was trying to, holding back her disappointment with effort. 'I—I——' she buried her face against his chest, clinging to him. 'No, I don't understand, Adam. I don't understand!' She pummelled her fists against him, hating him with each new blow.

'Natalie, *don't*! Please! Darling . . .' He held her hands pinned at her sides, claiming her mouth with a groan, silencing her with a savagery that took her breath away. When he at last raised his head they were both breathing heavily. 'When I'm with you like this I forget everything but possessing you, knowing every silken inch of your body,' he moaned.

'You already know it,' she teased throatily, having shared intimacies with this man that set her senses reeling.

His mouth quirked into a smile, the harsh man she had first met a week ago no longer in evidence, and she doubted he ever would be again for her. 'I do, don't I?' he agreed ruefully, sobering as he pinned her beneath him. 'Will you wait, Natalie?' he requested huskily. 'Until we have this affair with Judith and Jason out of the way?'

'To begin an affair of our own?' Her eyes glowed up at him, her legs entwined with his, the denim feeling rough against her bare skin.

'Will you?'

'Yes,' she nodded, knowing she could deny this man nothing. She didn't understand why Adam Thornton should be the man of her dreams, a man who evoked such a lack of inhibition within her. But he was, and she didn't intend fighting the attraction they had for each other. She wanted to *live* this, to flow with the desire, even welcomed the pain she knew would come in the end. Adam's suggestion of an affair had made it patently clear that he was no more in love with her than she was with him. It was an inexplicable desire, and she *wanted* it.

'Beautiful lady!' His arms tightened about her.

'Actually, I'm rather a cold lady at the moment,' she said in a quiet voice.

'Darling!' He laughed down at her, the warmth of his eyes totally banishing the frost Natalie had come to expect from him. 'I knew you were going to intrude into my life the first time I saw you.' He helped her put on the checked shirt, pulling her back down on to his chest as they talked.

'Why?' she snuggled against him.

'You were a complete surprise. I had no idea that the Natalie Faulkner I had to see looked anything like you,' he mused.

'Oh yes?'

'Fishing for compliments?'

'And if I am?' she quirked a mocking brow at him.

'You deserve them,' his hand caressed her thigh. 'You knocked me off balance the moment I saw you.'

'You did the same to me, but for a different reason,' she said tongue-in-cheek.

'Oh yes?' he taunted.

'You were arrogant, rude, and——'

'Don't!' Adam groaned in mock pain. 'You weren't what I was expecting. I had it in mind to read the riot act to some hard-headed witch of a woman, and instead you walked in, soft, feminine—and totally beddable,' he added with a taunting smile.

'Adam!' She gave him a playful thump on the chest.

'But you are—too much so.' He swung his legs to the floor, his expression grim. 'Once we've sorted out Jason and Judith we can concentrate on us.'

Natalie grimaced her horror, and came up on her knees next to him, her arms about his throat, the shirt reaching down to her thighs. 'Judith has another six months of her contract left with you!'

'I'm not waiting that long,' he told her firmly. 'Tracy will know the truth long before that.'

'You hope,' she added woefully.

'She will,' Adam pulled her forwards across his chest. 'I've never waited six months for any woman, and I'm not going to start with you.'

Natalie returned his kiss as he parted her lips, her arms clinging about his neck, only allowing herself to think of Adam's other women as he stood up to pull on his shirt. Adam was in his late thirties, had never been married, of course he had had other women, probably hundreds of them.

'What are you thinking?'

She looked up to find Adam frowning down at her. 'Nothing of importance,' she told him brightly.

'Natalie!' His tone was warning.

Her smile faltered and fell, her emotions open to this man who had stripped her of all the polished veneer it had taken her years to acquire. 'Are you very experienced?' she asked quietly.

He frowned, pausing in the action of pushing the bottom of his shirt into the black denims. 'Yes,' he bit out, turning away as he completed his task. 'Are you?'

'I—Well——' She was taken aback at the question. How could she admit to being a twenty-five-year-old virgin? *No one* was a twenty-five-year-old virgin! 'Not as much as you,' she evaded lightly. 'Maybe you could give me a few lessons?' she added teasingly, her bare legs long and shapely as she looked up at him impishly from her position on the sofa.

'Were you spanked as a child?' he mused.

She smiled, knowing his anger had gone. 'Not very often.'

'Then maybe you should have been.' He sat down beside her, his arm about her shoulders as he pulled her into him. 'Maybe I could administer a later reprimand,' he teased throatily against her temple.

'What did I do?' Natalie looked up at him innocently.

'You sat here looking like a little girl and boasted of your experience with other men,' he said with mock severity.

Her experience with other men! Adam was in for a shock when their affair did start!

'What are you thinking behind those mysterious eyes now?' he chided softly, watching the emotions flickering across her beautiful face, a glow surrounding her after their lovemaking.

She looked up at him beneath lowered lashes. 'I don't intend telling you *all* my secrets.'

'I'm going to know them all, Natalie,' Adam threatened lightly, pinching her chin just enough to cause a warning pain. 'In time,' he kissed her lingeringly on the mouth. 'You'll come to dinner on Saturday?' His dark gaze searched the beauty of her face.

She hid her disappointment that he didn't ask to see her tomorrow, nodding slowly. 'I do hope your sister likes me,' she frowned.

'She will,' he said with confidence, standing up to pull on his jacket. 'I'll have Jamieson pick you up. My chauffeur,' he explained at her puzzled frown.

'Oh, but couldn't you——'

'I'll be the host, Natalie,' he reminded her softly.

'Of course,' she flushed. 'Jamieson will be fine.'

'No, he won't.' Adam pulled her to her feet. 'But I'll make up for it once you get to my apartment.' He curved her against him, kissing her deeply, sighing his frustration as he leant his forehead on hers. 'I'll *more* than make up for it.' He put her firmly away from him. 'Jamieson will call for you at seven-fifteen.'

'I'll be ready,' she promised huskily.

'I'll be looking forward to seeing you.'

Natalie wanted to ask why he didn't arrange to see her tomorrow then if he wanted her that badly, but pride kept her silent as he took his leave of her, kissing her lightly on the lips.

Natalie made her way to bed slowly, lost in a dreamy euphoria, wishing she didn't have to go to bed alone, that Adam was with her. Maybe soon, very soon, he would be . . .

'Are you avoiding me?' Lester demanded to know.

Natalie had hardly been able to believe it when he turned up at her flat at seven o'clock Saturday evening. She was all ready for her evening out at Adam's, the dusty pink material of her cocktail dress interwoven with gold, giving a shimmering effect as she moved, her dark make-up deeply attractive, her hair a gleaming black bob.

When the doorbel had rung at seven o'clock she had thought it was Jamieson arriving early. She hadn't been able to hide her surprise, or dismay, when she saw it was Lester, and she invited him in dazedly. She hadn't seen him since the night they had gone to the theatre together, although she had received several telephone calls from him, turning down all his invitations. She had hardly expected him to just turn up here like this. Jamieson would be here at any moment!

'I'm going out, Lester,' she told him awkwardly.

'I can see that.' He looked at her with narrowed brown eyes. 'Anyone I know?'

'No,' she shook her head.

'Why, Natalie?' he frowned. 'I thought you liked me.'

'I do——'

'Then why?' he repeated angrily. 'I thought we had something good together. I was going to ask you to marry me, Natalie.'

She knew that. 'I'm not ready for marriage, Lester,' she told him lightly. 'Not with you or anyone else.'

'This man——'

'Is a friend, nothing more.' And yet she knew she lied. Adam could never be a friend to her, but oh, how she wanted him as a lover! She had spoken to him on the telephone yesterday afternoon, and even that had been enough to set her senses spinning, the eagerness with which he was looking forward to seeing her tonight echoed by her. Even now she could feel the excitement surging through her veins at the thought of shortly being with Adam again.

Lester frowned, his suspicion aroused by the dark flush to her cheeks. 'Are you sure about that?' he queried in a hurt voice.

'Lester, you really have no right——' She broke off as the doorbell rang. This time it had to be Jamieson!

Lester raised dark brows. 'Your date?'

'Er—yes.'

'Well, aren't you going to answer the door?' he taunted.

Her mouth set angrily. 'Of course.' She marched past him, pulling open the door, becoming flushed with embarrassment as Jamieson's curious gaze passed her to look on to Lester.

'Mr Thornton sent me, Miss Faulkner.' It was almost a question.

Her flush deepened. 'I'll be with you in just a moment,' she said dismissively.

Jamieson's censorious gaze returned to her. 'I'll wait downstairs, Miss Faulkner.'

'Thank you.' She was flustered as she closed the door to turn and collect her jacket and clutch-bag, giving Lester a pointed look.

'*Adam* Thornton?' he asked softly.

She sighed. 'Yes.'

'Business or pleasure, Natalie?'

Her head went back, her irritation acute. 'A little of both,' she told him defiantly.

'I see.' His mouth twisted. 'Well, don't let me delay you,' and he walked to the door.

He had gone before she could make any further comment. Damn him! He had already taken some of the gloss out of the evening, making her feel almost guilty for wanting to see Adam. And why should she feel guilty? Adam made her feel marvellously alive, wonderfully happy. She was going to enjoy this evening with him in spite of Lester.

Jamieson got out of the car to open the back door for her the moment she came down the steps, seeing that she was comfortable before getting back behind the wheel. The back of the car smelt vaguely of the cheroots Adam liked to smoke, bringing the memory of him to her vividly. She hoped Tracy and Jason hadn't already arrived; she would like to be alone with Adam for a few minutes at least. Certainly long enough for him to kiss her.

Once they reached the apartment building Jamieson once more got out to open the door of the Rolls for her, and Natalie looked up at the apartment building with something like awe, not liking to even guess how many storeys it was.

'Mr Thornton has the penthouse apartment, Miss Faulkner,' the chauffeur supplied.

'Thank you,' she said gratefully, wondering how she was going to find that out without appearing too stupid. She had no idea where Adam lived.

The man on the desk showed her into the lift himself. The inside of the building had a quiet elegance that spoke of opulence. The lift doors opened directly into Adam's apartment, and Adam himself stood only a short distance away from her as the door closed behind her and the lift began its descent. He looked magnificent, the deep blue of his velvet dinner jacket deepening the colour of his eyes, emphasising the height and breadth of him, the darkness of his hair, the distinguished grey at his temples.

Natalie noticed none of the warmth and style of the room as she continued to look at him, not the deep pile carpet of the dark brown carpet, the goatskin scatter rugs, the tan leather suite, the tasteful paintings on the pale green walls, the beautiful brown velvet curtains, the drinks unit and mahogany stereo, soft music filtering from the latter. She had eyes only for Adam, not even noticing as the butler took her jacket, only moving forward as Adam took a step towards her.

'What was he doing there, Natalie?' Adam stood directly in front of her, almost touching her, but not quite.

Her brain felt befuddled by his closeness. 'Who?' she echoed dazedly. 'Where?'

'Lester,' he bit out, his eyes narrowed. 'What was he doing at your flat?'

She frowned. 'How did you——'

'Jamieson used the telephone in the car to tell me

he'd been delayed because you had a—visitor. It was Lester, wasn't it?' he demanded to know.

'Yes. But—You're hurting me, Adam!' she gasped as his fingers bit painfully into her arms.

'Are you still seeing him?' he rasped.

'No——'

'Then why was he there?'

'He just came to see why I didn't want to go out with him any more. Adam, you're *hurting* me!' she repeated with a groan.

Still he didn't relent, his eyes glittering down at her. 'I'd hate to think you're like your sister after all.'

Natalie bristled resentfully at this unfounded condemnation. 'What are you implying?'

'I believe you already know that,' he bit out.

She drew in an angry breath, her pleasure at seeing him again rapidly dissolving in the face of his accusations. 'I don't think I——'

'*Hell*, why are we thinking at all!' he groaned suddenly, pulling her hard against his body, claiming her mouth with his, his fierceness knocking the breath from her lungs.

She rebelled at his rough handling, still angry with him, then she felt the warmth entering her body, reaching out and touching every part of her, so that soon she abandoned herself to standing on tiptoe to return the kiss, her arms about his neck.

'Mm, that was good!' Adam breathed his satisfaction several minutes later. 'I believe we were about to have our first argument,' he mused, still holding her firmly in the circle of his arms.

'First?' she derided, her heartbeat seeming to take for ever to steady to normal.

'The others were different,' he shrugged dismissal of them. 'Then I didn't know what you mean to me.'

She still didn't know, and she wasn't going to find

out just now, because the ascent of the lift told her that Tracy and Jason had arrived and were on their way up.

'Don't be nervous,' Adam kissed her lightly as he sensed her tension. 'You'll be fine.'

She turned to greet the other couple as the lift doors opened, instantly recognising Jason Dillman, the blond good looks almost too good to be true, the sure confidence in dark brown eyes. He looked surprised to see her, which meant Adam hadn't seen fit to tell him she was to be here tonight. Before she could turn her full attention on the woman at his side she was shocked to the core by Adam's method of introduction.

'Jason you already know, Natalie. And this is my sister Tracy. Tracy, this is my hostess and—and friend, Natalie Faulkner.'

Natalie looked up at him in amazement, his arm still about her shoulders as he obliquely laid claim to a relationship he had turned down from her only two days ago, that of being her lover!

CHAPTER SIX

NATALIE acknowledged the introductions as if in a dream, alone now as Adam poured drinks for the other couple, the butler having taken Tracy's wrap. Natalie could feel the colour slowly flooding her cheeks as she received curious looks from both Tracy and Jason, the latter mockingly so; there was a slight leer to the brown eyes she deliberately avoided.

Adam had deliberately given the impression that she was the latest woman in his life, and while that could have become true two nights ago she didn't like the way he had laid claim to the relationship in front of the other couple.

She accepted her drink from him, determinedly ignoring him and turning her attention to Tracy Dillman. It was obvious the two of them were brother and sister; the colouring was the same, the blue eyes and very dark hair, but the harshness and cynicism shown in the brother's eyes and mouth were softened out to an incredible, almost unbelievable beauty in the sister. Tracy's features were so softly delicate she looked almost unreal.

Natalie dealt with beautifully sophisticated and polished women every day, women who could rate as some of the most beautiful in the world; Judith's perfect features were a good example of that. And yet Tracy Dillman had an ethereal beauty, the sort of delicately etched features that haunted.

Natalie watched the other woman as she spoke to Adam, admired her natural grace, every movement seeming to be one of beauty, her laugh like the melodious tinkling of a bell as her brother said something funny. Tracy was exquisite, almost childlike at times, having an eagerness, a vivaciousness that gave her inner sparkle, the fresh alertness of her expression seeming to show her interest in everything. She had the look of an entranced child, still believing in all the promise and magic life had to offer, had a magnetic beauty that drew people to her, one minute looking the child, the next a sensually exciting woman as she unconsciously flirted with deeply blue eyes and long dark lashes.

Looking at her, witnessing her bubbly happiness that seemed to charm the people about her, Natalie found it difficult to understand why Jason needed other woman, why he had Judith now. And Tracy obviously adored her husband; she touched him often, her fingers caressing, so why did Jason have affairs?

By Adam's scowl in his brother-in-law's direction she would say his thoughts were running along the same lines, although Jason seemed oblivious of the disapproval of either of them, as he seemed unaware of his wife's loving expression, drinking heavily of the whisky Adam's butler was now at hand to supply him with every time his glass looked like emptying. Natalie was still sipping her first glass of sherry, Jason was probably on his fourth glass of whisky.

Brother and sister chatted—at least, Tracy did, seemingly unaware of the tense atmosphere about her, and Natalie felt resentful of Adam's introductory words of possessiveness, and the way his hand firmly held her elbow. Jason was lost in his own private lack of interest in his surroundings.

'I had no idea you were holding out for the head of the company.'

She turned sharply at the scorn in those softly spoken words, realising the reason for Jason's insulting behaviour as she saw that the brother and sister were now intent on Adam's extensive record collection, leaving her momentarily open to Jason's barbs.

She gave him a haughty look, her training as a model allowing her to withstand the familiarity of his gaze as he openly looked down the low cleavage of her gown. 'I beg your pardon?' she enquired coolly.

'Adam,' he sneered. 'The powerful head of Thornton Cosmetics. You would have got further with me, Natalie,' he smiled, shaking his head. 'Adam doesn't give favours for privileges.'

'No?' She arched dark brows.

His confidence wasn't shaken in the least by her coolness. 'No,' he affirmed. 'Whereas I . . .'

Her contempt was obvious as she looked at him. 'I'm well aware of your business practices—as is Adam,' she added pointedly.

He was still unshaken, glancing over to where his wife was now laughing happily with her brother, her long dark hair falling in soft waves to just below her shoulders in a lightly feathered style that added thickness and vitality to its glowing blackness. But Jason seemed to see none of his wife's magnetic pull, as he looked at his brother-in-law. 'As is Adam,' he confirmed lightly.

She gasped. 'Don't you care?'

Jason smiled. 'Adam has known of my—practice, for seven years,' he drawled. 'Why should I start to care now?'

'You unfeeling swine!'

'And Judith told me you were the calm, practical one!' he taunted.

Oh, how she hated this man! He cared for no one but himself, not his wife, and certainly not for the over-confident Judith. He would use her sister, and when she bored him or became a nuisance, he would discard her, as he would have done Tracy long ago—if only she weren't so useful to him in her trusting love.

Her mouth twisted contemptuously. 'I'm calm and practical enough to see straight through you!'

'And Adam?'

Natalie hated herself for the blush in her cheeks, but she didn't think any woman would completely control the dull red colour—especially as a lot of it was due to anger! If Tracy Dillman weren't here, a sweetly naïve woman who seemed blind to the darker side of her husband's nature, she couldn't have hesitated to tell this man exactly what she thought of him.

As it was, she could only glare at him, the aquamarine colour of her eyes lightening to green. 'My relationship with Adam is none of your damned business!' she snapped.

'Maybe not,' he taunted. 'But I'm sure Judith will be interested to hear that her supposedly prudish sister has no need to preach after all.'

Natalie stiffened, her eyes narrowed. 'What do you mean?'

He gave a mocking laugh, his good-looking face ugly in his contempt. 'Judith told me about the sisterly chats the two of you have been having lately, about your preaching attitude. She was even starting to feel guilty about seeing me, but not when I've told her about you and Adam.'

Her mouth tightened. 'Told her what?'

He continued to smile, the expression in his eyes deliberately insolent as her breasts heaved up and down beneath the pink and gold material of her dress, her anger acute. 'I'm not blinded to you by sisterly respect as Judith is,' he taunted. 'I can see exactly why you've chosen to share Adam's bed.'

'Really?' Her tone was icy.

Jason nodded. 'Adam's really angry this time, he

must be to have threatened Judith. I'm proud of the way she threatened him straight back!' he added with relish.

And Natalie could cheerfully have hit her sister in that moment for telling this man so much! Judith had to be completely infatuated with him. 'Even though your wife could be hurt by such a threat?' she snapped.

'Tracy?' he glanced over at her. 'She wouldn't believe it,' he said with satisfaction. 'You may have noticed, Tracy is in love with me.'

'Yes,' she sighed.

'Don't look so disgusted, Natalie,' he mocked. 'We all do what we have to to survive in this life. I need other women, you need your agency. And you're willing to do anything you can to give it the success it deserves.'

Angry colour darkened her cheeks, her eyes glittering with suppressed fury. 'I don't like your implication,' she ground out.

'No?' Jason arched one dark blond brow. 'You should have thought of that before you took Adam as your lover.'

'I——'

'Didn't either of you hear Morton announce dinner?' Adam had joined them without either of them being aware of it, his blue eyes narrowed suspiciously.

Jason smiled at him, a leering smile that owed little to genuine humour. 'Don't worry,' he drawled. 'Your—friend and I have merely been discussing mutual business acquaintances.'

'Indeed?' The other man looked sceptical.

'Oh, but we have, haven't we, Natalie?'

She glared her dislike at him. His conversation might have been extremely insulting, but it was true that Judith and Adam, the main topics of their conversation, were business acquaintances of them both. 'Yes,' she confirmed tightly.

'How interesting,' Adam drawled with heavy sarcasm. 'If you'll excuse us, Jason . . .?' he said pointedly.

The other man shrugged, moving to join Tracy as they went into the dining-room.

Natalie walked at Adam's side, staring straight ahead as Jason saw his wife seated at the table, knowing that piercing blue eyes never left her profile.

'Did Jason insult you?' Adam rasped at her continued silence.

Still she didn't look at him. 'Wasn't he supposed to?'

His fingers bit into her arm. 'What the hell is that supposed to mean?'

Now Natalie did look at him, her eyes sending out darts of bitter anger. 'Did you expect your brother-in-law to *respect* your "friend"?' she bit out furiously.

'By that I take it he didn't?'

'No!'

'I see.' His eyes were like chips of ice as he pulled out her chair for her to sit down, seating himself opposite her at the oval table, Jason to one side of him, Tracy the other.

Like their lord and master, Natalie thought bitterly as she accepted the chilled melon placed in front of her. The conversation for the main part passed over her, although she noticed Adam was very terse towards Jason, a fact the other man recognised with an amused and triumphant smile in her direction.

'Natalie?'

She looked up to find Tracy watching her curiously, a dull red tinge entering her cheeks as she realised the other woman must have been talking to her for some minutes—and she hadn't heard a word! She should have known this evening was going to be a disaster when Lester had arrived at her flat so unexpectedly. It had only got worse!

'Sorry?' She plastered an over-bright smile to her lips, forcing a look of interest to her face.

Tracy smiled, bearing no chagrin for Natalie's inattentiveness. 'I was just saying how exciting it must be to head an agency like yours,' she repeated with quiet sincerity.

'Oh, Natalie—works very hard,' Jason put in softly.

Natalie drew in an angry breath, her knuckles showing white as she clenched her hands. 'I——'

'She's very important—to the company,' Adam put in with quiet intensity, the double edge to his words missed by no one, except maybe Tracy, who looked so innocently naïve at the moment that Natalie doubted she even knew the meaning of the word innuendo.

But Jason didn't miss it, and for the first time this evening he looked disconcerted, frowning at Adam, finding his gaze met in arrogant challenge. Finally it was the younger man's gaze that fell.

'It must be very exciting being a model.' Tracy's face glowed as she completely missed that moment of tension.

'Hard work,' Natalie smiled at the other woman's enthusiasm.

'Were you ever a model?'

'Once,' she nodded.

'Did you like it?'

'Yes. But I like being an agent better.'

'I suppose——'

'Really, darling,' Jason drawled mockingly, 'don't bore Natalie with your ceaseless questions!'

Natalie could quite cheerfully have hit him for the way Tracy momentarily lost all her sparkle, and her expression turned fleetingly wistful, hauntingly so as she changed from a beautiful woman to an unsure little girl.

Adam's mouth tightened, and he set about charming his young sister from the sudden mood of melancholy she had drifted into because of her husband's sharpness.

Natalie joined in their conversation now and again,

although Jason remained triumphantly silent as his young wife tried in vain to get back into his favour. Natalie's dislike of the man grew as the evening progressed, so much so that she wondered how Adam kept his hands off him. Jason Dillman had to be the most obnoxious man she had ever met—and Tracy had to be one of the *sweetest* people she had ever met. What a mess! If only Tracy didn't love her husband so much, Jason and Judith certainly seemed to deserve each other; both of them were selfish in the extreme. The two of them would surely destroy each other in the end.

As Adam feared Jason would destroy Tracy before he was finished with her! She could now understand his concern for his sister, and she echoed that concern after having met Tracy.

Tracy smiled at her as she and Jason took their leave shortly after eleven. 'I hope we meet again,' she said with a sincerity that couldn't be doubted.

Natalie was once again aware of Adam's possessive arm about her waist as they stood at the door as the other couple took their leave; she knew by the tension about his mouth as he glanced down at her that he was totally aware of the tactics she had used to avoid contact or conversation with him all evening. She was still furiously angry about his arrogant claim to a relationship with her, and she had no intention of letting him get away with such a liberty.

'I'm sure you will,' Adam assured his sister smoothly.

Tracy's eyes widened with understanding. 'Maybe the two of you could come to dinner with us one evening?'

'I——'

'We would like that. Wouldn't we, Natalie?' He looked down at her warningly.

She nodded wordlessly, hating him with her eyes, and knowing he knew of her resentment.

'I'll call you, shall I?' Tracy suggested to her brother. 'I think that would be best,' he nodded.

Natalie moved away from him as soon as the other couple had left, slipping out of the arc of his arm to face him rebelliously. 'Could you ask Morton for my jacket too, please,' she said stiffly.

Adam moved to pour himself a whisky, his eyes narrowed at her over the rim of his glass. 'You aren't leaving,' he stated calmly, his gaze challenging.

Her mouth tightened. 'But I am.'

'No,' he shook his head, the glass landing on the table with a resounding thud as he came towards her. 'We haven't finished our conversation yet.'

He was towering over her, totally daunting, and yet she refused to be intimidated. 'Which conversation is that?' she met his challenge, her gaze unflinching. 'The one about how I'm your woman, and everyone is going to know it?' Her voice shook over the latter, her anger making her tremble with reaction.

'Natalie——'

'But we didn't even start the conversation, Adam,' she bit out furiously. 'I certainly never agreed to it.'

'Didn't you?' he taunted harshly. 'I had the distinct impression the other evening that being my woman was exactly what you'd agreed to.'

She breathed shakily. 'That was unfair!'

He sighed his impatience. 'What else was I supposed to tell them, Natalie?' he demanded. 'That you're just a business acquaintance?'

'Why not?' Her eyes flashed. 'It's the truth.'

'Is it?'

'Yes!' she flushed at his derision.

Adam shook his head, his exasperation a tangible force. 'Then who was the woman who pleaded with me to make love to her two days ago? I'm sure it was the same woman I kissed so passionately only three hours ago.'

'That was before——' She broke off, chewing on her bottom lip.

'Before . . .?' he prompted hardly.

'Before you introduced me so—so *intimately* to your sister and Jason,' she muttered reluctantly.

'I introduced you as a friend——'

'And we all know what that means!'

'Do we?' His eyes were narrowed.

'Don't be so dense, Adam,' she snapped. 'Men like you don't have woman friends.'

The blue eyes glittered dangerously. 'Men like me?' he repeated softly.

She swallowed hard, knowing by the grim set of his jaw that Adam was very angry too now. She sighed. 'I didn't mean it like that——'

'Then how the hell did you mean it?' he rasped. 'I introduced you as a friend, you take exception to it. Are you a woman or a child, Natalie?'

'I'm a woman!' she flushed.

'Then damn well act like one. Are you ashamed of the attraction we have for each other, is that it?' His mouth twisted. 'Do you usually choose men like Lester, men who think themselves lucky to be allowed to touch you?'

'And don't boast of it, you mean?' she accused heatedly.

Adam became strangely still, his narrowed eyes icy cold as his gaze ripped into her. 'Are you saying that's what I did?'

Natalie drew in a ragged breath. 'You certainly let them know what role I play in your life!'

'You're becoming hysterical——'

'And you're damned arrogant!' Natalie glared at him, her breasts heaving in her agitation. 'Now, I'd like to leave.'

'Don't worry, I'll get your jacket so that you can do

just that.' Adam rang for the butler. 'One thing about "men like me",' he ground out, 'is that we never keep a woman against her will.'

She flushed at the barb of his tone, turning away as he asked the butler to bring her jacket.

What a disaster of an evening! She had anticipated this time together since they had parted Thursday evening, and now they were parting like strangers.

Adam tersely dismissed the butler after he had brought her jacket, holding it out to her himself, moving slowly round her to pull the lapels together.

Natalie swallowed hard, looking up at him with eyes swimming in tears, then saw his expression soften, the harshness go out of his eyes.

'For Pete's sake, woman,' he groaned, 'let's not have our second argument!'

'I think we've already had it,' she said miserably.

'Do you really want to leave?' He cupped either side of her face with his hands.

'No,' she admitted huskily.

'I think the only way to stop us arguing is for me to kiss you,' his head lowered.

Natalie welcomed the warmth of his mouth, instantly melting against him, feeling the surge of his body as his hardening thighs told of his arousal.

His lips moved to the warm throb of her throat. 'Do you still mind being thought my woman?' he teased softly.

From the moment his mouth had touched hers she had felt that familiar melting feeling, had wondered if she couldn't be a little in love with this man after all. But his teasing tone didn't rob the words of the truth. If she ever allowed Adam to make love to her she would just be another of his women, discarded when she no longer held his attention. As the Princess had been . . .?

'What is it, darling?' Adam frowned down at her.

'Let me go,' she ordered coldly.

'Natalie——'

'I'd like to go now.'

'What the hell did I say or do now?' he burst out impatiently.

'Nothing.' She pulled her jacket more comfortably about her shoulders. 'It's late, I'd like to leave.'

'Perverse woman,' he rasped, shrugging. 'Okay, let's go. I'm not in the mood to play the games you seem intent on.'

Her eyes flashed. 'I'm sure your *other* women don't play such games.'

'So that's it,' he sighed. 'I'll answer my own question of earlier—you're a child, Natalie. And it's time you were tucked up in your virtuous little bed.' He picked up some car keys from the hall table, his intention obvious.

'I—But—Jamieson?' she frowned her consternation, not welcoming being alone with him on the drive to her home.

His mouth twisted. 'At home with his family long ago. I'll drive you myself.'

Not the Rolls this time but the silver Porsche she had seen that first day she had visited Adam at his office. The sleekly lined car ate up the miles to her home in no time at all.

Natalie sat as far away from Adam as she could get in the confines of the car, knowing that all the accusations he had levelled at her were true. The liberated woman of two days ago had taken a hard knock the moment she knew being his 'friend' meant being known as his mistress, having people like Jason Dillman know that. Having to withstand his insults had more than brought home to her the precariousness of such a relationship. If that meant she was still a child then she didn't dispute the fact, she accepted being the coward that made her. She wasn't ready to be anyone's mistress, not even a man she desired as much as Adam Thornton.

And she did desire him. She just wasn't ready to commit herself to a relationship that had no commitments for her in return.

She had no idea they had reached her home until Adam leant past her to unlock her door, pushing it open from the inside. Natalie had recoiled as soon as his arm brushed against her breasts, her gaze dropping from his as she saw contempt in the blue depths.

Adam sat back in his seat. 'Goodnight, Natalie,' he said distantly. 'I'll be in touch.'

'Our—bargain still stands?' She wetted her lips nervously with the tip of her tongue.

'Yes,' he bit out, his foot pressing down impatiently on the accelerator of the powerful car, revving up the engine pointedly.

'Adam——'

'Just go, Natalie,' he sighed. 'We'll talk again when you're feeling more—sensible.'

More adult, he meant, and she knew it. Oh, why couldn't she be more like Judith, why cling to her virginity like a talisman? Her sister had lost her virginity to a summer acquaintance when she was only seventeen, and she didn't seem to regret it for a moment. How ridiculous that her own capitulation to a man should have to mean more. And yet it did.

With the perversity of the woman Adam had accused her of being Natalie wanted him to call her all the next day, kept expecting the telephone or the doorbell to ring. But it didn't, and she couldn't exactly blame Adam, in fact she couldn't blame him at all. And maybe it was better this way. Maybe . . .

She took advantage of her suddenly empty day to do

more *work on the folder she had prepared for a proposed Fantasy Girl, reassessing the three girls she had already picked out, but she now felt a dissatisfaction with them all. A fantasy girl should be exactly that, a woman of complete fantasy, and while all her models were beautiful, none of them quite seemed to fit the description of a fantasy girl. Still, she wasn't going to be the one to make such an important decision, she only had to submit the most suitable models she had. Adam had the hard part.

Dee was already in the office when Natalie arrived the next day. 'Have a good weekend?' she asked curiously.

'Fine, thanks,' she answered absently, knowing she hadn't spent such a terrible weekend in a long time.

Dee frowned, saying no more as Natalie went through to her office. But she wasn't deceived by Natalie's nonchalant air for a moment, knew that the ecstatic glow of Friday had gone. Had Adam Thornton also gone . . .?

Natalie was wondering the same thing herself as she sat behind her desk. Adam had said their bargain still stood, but she knew their own friendship, brief as it had been, was over.

And she was so miserable about it. She was a twenty-five-year-old virgin, something as outdated as the liberty bodice, and she was likely to stay that way too if she carried on the way she was doing. If only she dared tell Adam she was sorry! But he had made his disgust with her obvious, had probably spent last night in the Princess's arms. Pride held her back from telephoning him.

Mid-morning he telephoned her.

Dee buzzed through to her just after eleven. 'It's him, Natalie,' she said breathlessly. 'Want to talk to him?'

Natalie had instantly tensed. 'Who is he, Dee?' she

delayed, knowing exactly who it was but needing time to compose herself.

Her friend laughed. 'It could only be one man—Adam Thornton!'

That was what she had thought, and his temper wouldn't have been improved by this delay.

It wasn't. 'I want to see you, Natalie,' he told her abruptly as soon as Dee had put him through.

'Well, I——'

'This is business, Natalie,' he bit out, his leashed anger just as effective over the telephone.

She stiffened. 'I didn't think it was anything else,' she said tartly.

'Didn't you?'

'No!'

'I wish it was,' Adam snapped.

'Adam——'

'Can you come over here now?' he asked tersely. 'And bring some possible Fantasy Girls with you. Photographs, not the girls themselves,' he derided. 'We may have to bring the publicity forward on it.'

Natalie's interest quickened. 'May I ask why?'

'No, you may not. Just get over here, now. I'll expect you in twenty minutes.'

'But I——'

'Twenty minutes, Natalie,' and the receiver was slammed down the other end.

Arrogant man! She could have any number of other appointments this morning, and he would expect her to break them all so that she could go and see him. And didn't he have a right to expect just that? Yes, damn him, he did!

Her anger was increased as she saw the knowing gleam in Dee's eyes as she told her where she was going. Dee was much too astute not to have noticed how deeply attracted Natalie had become to their most important client.

This time Natalie wasn't kept waiting at all, but was shown straight into Adam's office. Adam allowed no time for more than cursory greetings, demanding the folder she had with her and instantly becoming immersed in its contents. Thank goodness she had had the forethought to get the file ready!

While Adam studied each girl thoroughly Natalie had time to study him, to once again feel that stirring of her senses to this vibrantly alive man, her fingers aching to lace themselves into the dark thickness of his hair, to run down the rigid hardness of his jaw, to know the muscled firmness of his body against hers.

Suddenly he looked up and caught her softened gaze on him, his brows raising questioningly at the hot colour that flooded her cheeks. She turned away sharply before he could read the desire in her eyes.

He closed the file with a snap. 'None of these women are suitable,' he dismissed harshly.

'None?' she grimaced, dismayed that he should think the same as she did. And if he should decide that none of her models were suitable then she would lose the contract for Fantasy Girl anyway. She moved quickly to his side, bending forward to open the file, her perfume soft and elusive. 'What about Joanna? I thought——' She had made the mistake of looking down at him, finding herself dangerously close to him, unable to resist that urge now, her hand coming up almost of its own volition to caress the hardness of his cheek.

His gaze held hers, but he didn't touch her. 'What did you think?' he asked huskily.

'I thought—I—Oh, Adam,' she groaned. 'Adam, I——'

'Well, I've found *my* fantasy girl!' His arms came fiercely about her as he pulled her down on to him, his mouth claiming and parting hers as he knocked down the last of her barriers, her sigh of capitulation swallowed up in the savage sweetness of the kiss.

Natalie buried her face shyly in his throat as he looked down at her with unleashed desire. 'I've been so stupid,' she murmured against the warmth of his skin. 'Forgive me?'

'Anything!' He kissed her again until her lips clung to his. 'I ought to beat you for the hell you've put me through the last couple of days!' He rested his damp forehead on hers as she lay across his chest.

'I thought the Princess might have consoled you?' Her teasing was made in the form of a question.

'I think I *will* beat you for that!' Adam scowled.

Relief flooded her heart. 'You mean she didn't console you?'

'No, she damn well didn't! I haven't seen Maria since the evening you saw us together at the theatre. Now apologise—in a suitable manner,' he growled.

'Suitable?' she teased, feeling so happy she was lightheaded.

'Do it, woman!'

Her lips on his held nothing back, and she could feel the answering surge in his body as he crushed her to him.

'Tonight, Natalie,' he murmured against her mouth. 'I can't wait any longer than that.'

'Come to dinner,' she invited breathlessly, never doubting his answer, and never doubting her own either. All her doubts, all her arguments of Saturday ceased to matter. Adam was all that mattered, because she had found all the commitment she needed. She *loved* him.

CHAPTER SEVEN

NATALIE didn't attempt to analyse it; she knew that would achieve nothing. She was ecstatically, irrevocably in love with Adam Thornton, and knowing that made a mockery of any need for commitment from him. She would accept what little he was prepared to give, for as long as he was prepared to give it.

When the three dozen white roses arrived at the office for her later that afternoon she didn't need to read the card with them to know who they were from. She couldn't help smiling once she had read the message in that bold black handwriting, putting through a call to Adam straight away.

'I haven't changed my mind,' she told him the moment he came on the line. 'So your sanity is perfectly intact.'

'Good.'

'Do you like steak?' she enquired happily.

'Anything will be fine.'

'You can have me for dessert,' she smiled at the thought.

'Good.'

For the first time she became aware of his lack of response to her teasing. 'Adam, do you have someone with you?' she frowned.

'Yes,' he answered with some relief.

She laughed wickedly, lightheaded with happiness. 'How interesting! I have this amazing black dress I'm going to wear this evening, it has no back, virtually no front, and a slit right up——'

'Natalie!' he warned in an agonised voice.

'Too much for you, darling?' she mocked.

'At this particular time, yes.' His voice was once again businesslike.

'And later?'

'I'm looking forward to it.' There was a definite threat in his tone now.

'So am I,' she laughed before ringing off, and she was still smiling when Dee came into the room.

The other woman looked wistfully at the roses, each bloom a delicate bud just longing to bloom. Rather like Natalie herself! And Adam would be her sunlight.

'Everything all right again now?' Dee looked down at her.

Natalie blushed. 'Yes.'

Her friend shook her head ruefully. 'When you fall in love it's supposed to be the end of all the uncertainties— it's usually just the beginning,' she grimaced. 'After three years I still don't know all Tom's complexities. But it's half the fun finding them out,' she laughed.

Yes, it was. And it could take for ever to know a man like Adam. She didn't have that long, but she would make the most of what she did have.

Adam arrived promptly at seven-thirty that evening, with yet more roses, dozens and dozens of them.

'I've already run out of vases,' she laughed happily, her eyes glowing.

'Then put them in the bath,' he dismissed the expensive blooms. 'They were only in case you might have changed your mind since this afternoon. I didn't think you'd throw out a man who bought you flowers.'

She moved into his arms. 'I'm not usually that mercenary,' she told him huskily. 'It was just that——'

'I was too damned arrogant on Saturday night,' he finished firmly. 'It hadn't occurred to me that you'd take exception to the way I introduced you to Tracy and Jason.'

'Is that because most of your women are proud of that fact?' she teased.

'Natalie!'

She gurgled with laughter. 'I was being very silly the other evening, and——'

His gentle fingertips on her lips stopped further self-condemnation. 'You were yourself, and I'm glad of it. I respect you more than any other woman I've ever known,' he told her softly.

She blinked back the tears, knowing that with a cynical man like Adam respect was a rare emotion for him to feel. She felt honoured that he bestowed such feelings on her. 'I'm glad,' she smiled shakily.

He moved back, grinning to break the sudden mood of intensity. 'Now where is that sexy black dress I've been torturing myself with all day?'

Humour curved her own lips. The midnight-blue dress she wore clung to her slender curves, but was certainly nowhere near as revealing as the black creation she had described to him over the telephone. 'You wouldn't really expect me to wear a dress like that, Adam?' she smiled.

'I was looking forward to it.'

'But I don't even possess a dress like that!'

'I'll buy you one,' he promised indulgently. 'For my eyes only.'

She still smiled, but a shadow had passed over her face. 'I don't want this to spoil the evening,' she said slowly. 'And I don't want you to be angry.' She smoothed the frown from his brow that had been gathering. 'Flowers I like—although maybe not quite so many of them,' she smiled. 'But anything else ... I don't need it, Adam.'

'I'm not trying to buy you. I'd like to buy you *things*.'

'I know that,' she nodded. 'And I'm thrilled that you would like to. But——'

'Don't,' he finished ruefully.

'No,' she confirmed.

'You're a difficult woman to please,' he frowned.

'Not difficult,' she shook her head. 'Just give of yourself, Adam. That's all I want.'

Something like pain flickered across his hard features. 'I don't understand you.'

'You will,' she promised. 'You will!'

The rest of the evening passed in a dream for Natalie. The meal was cooked to perfection, the wine Adam had brought with him was perfect too, and the softly romantic music coming from the stereo added to the mood.

They sat side by side on the sofa, Adam enjoying an after-dinner cheroot with his brandy, Natalie curled up at his side.

Suddenly he turned to her. 'Why did you stop seeing Lester?'

She frowned her puzzlement at his interest. 'Adam . . .?'

He turned to her completely, stubbing out the cheroot to clasp her shoulders with compelling hands. 'I need to know, Natalie. I'm trying to know *you*.'

'Don't you already know me?'

'Unfortunately, no. Why did you stop seeing him, Natalie?'

She shrugged. 'Because he wanted me to be one of those women you're trying so hard to stop Tracy being. No matter how much I—I loved a man,' her voice lowered huskily, 'I could never be a stay-at-home wife. I need my career. I love it.'

'Did you love Lester?'

She met his gaze steadily, all her love for *him* shining in her eyes as she heard his breath catch in his throat. 'No,' she told him unnecessarily, knowing she had given herself away irrevocably.

'Dear heavens, Natalie!' He bent her back against the cushions, parting her lips, seeking the inner warmth of her mouth. 'When I'm with you I forget whether it's night or day. I forget everything but you!' he groaned into her throat.

'Darling,' she caressed his nape. 'I'll help you with Tracy,' she promised. 'If you'll let me.'

'Tracy . . .?' She knew by the dazed expression in his eyes that he had forgotten his own sister! 'We'll both help Tracy,' he nodded grimly. 'But right now you've got to help me!'

'Help you . . .?'

'Make love to me, Natalie,' he pleaded shakily, totally unlike the self-assured man who had arrived at her flat three hours ago, his black silk shirt unbuttoned down his chest, his cream jacket discarded altogether, 'Stop this burning ache I have to possess you!'

The next hour was a time of wonderment and discovery for Natalie, Adam's lovemaking knew no boundaries as he aroused her to the same peak of desire he didn't hide from her, arousing her so deeply and so thoroughly that when the time came for his body to join with hers she knew no pain, only pleasure.

But Adam's body instantly gentled on hers, as if some inner knowledge had told him of her inexperience, building the sensations slowly so as not to frighten or alarm her, controlling her and himself until they reached the earth-shattering climax together, spiralling over the edge of the world, it seemed to Natalie.

A drugging tiredness invaded her body, a need for sleep like she had never known before. 'I love you,' she told him sleepily before snuggling into his throat to fall into a satiated and dreamless sleep.

Some time towards morning she awoke to find herself held in Adam's arms, the strength of his embrace telling her he had no intention of releasing her, although the even rise and fall of his chest showed him to be asleep. With a sigh of contentment Natalie went back to sleep in his arms.

The next time she woke it was morning, and the bright sunshine of a warm autumn day was streaming in at the window. And she was alone in the bed, only the warmth of the sheets next to her telling her that Adam had only recently got out of the bed.

As she sat up with the intention of searching for him he came into the room, wearing only his black trousers, the tanned hardness of his chest bearing the mark of her nails as she had experienced the aching pleasure of fulfilment. She blushed at such tangible evidence of her abandonment, and her gaze shifted to his face, seeing by the clean strength of his jaw and the dampness of his hair that he had already showered and shaved.

'Your bath awaits, my lady,' he teased softly, his expression somewhat wary to her sensitive gaze.

'My bath?' she frowned.

'Mm.' He threw back the sheet that had been their only covering during the night, and scooped her up into his arms to look down at her concernedly. 'Was I gentle enough with you?' he asked huskily as he carried her through to the adjoining bathroom.

Now she knew the reason for his wariness, his concern. Adam knew she had been a virgin last night. 'I'm not ashamed, Adam.' She looked up at him fearlessly.

His expression darkened. 'You have no need to be!'

She looked away. 'And you have no need to feel— responsible,' she told him softly. 'About anything.'

Adam smiled as he placed her in the warmth of the water he had prepared for her, kneeling down to pick up the perfumed soap and began washing her body. 'Oh, but I am responsible,' he mused. 'I have a deep— and intense responsibility to your body,' his hands moved soapily over the softness of her breasts, causing the nipples to harden invitingly. 'And I intend to continue being—responsible, for it.' He looked at her, suddenly serious. 'Do you mind?'

She smiled shyly. He didn't regret making love to her, didn't mind that she had been a virgin! 'I don't mind at all,' she glowed.

'Thank goodness for that! Are all the aches out of your body now?'

'Yes. But——'

'I need you again.' He swept her back up into his arms, unconcerned with her wetness.

If anything it was even better than the night before. Natalie knew better how to please him today, feeling no inhibitions as she knew she gave him pleasure in return for all the passion he showered on her.

It was after ten by the time they went down to Adam's Porsche, and neither of them seemed to give a thought to the fact that they should both have been in their offices over an hour ago.

'I'll pick you up at five-thirty,' Adam told her after she had refused to have lunch with him, claiming she couldn't possibly take a lunch-break when she was in so late. 'And then we can—Hell, I forgot about Tracy's invitation,' he scowled. 'She wants us to go to dinner tonight, and I accepted. And I forgot to tell you last night.'

Natalie hid her disappointment well; she did not want to share him with anyone at the moment, she wanted him all to herself. But she had promised to help him with Tracy, and she would do just that. 'Your memory is going, darling,' she teased him, seeing desire flare in his eyes as she lightly caressed his cheek.

He bent forward and kissed her fiercely on the mouth. 'What did you say?' he murmured raggedly a few minutes later.

'You see?' she laughed throatily. 'Poor Adam!'

'Poor Adam, indeed,' he pretended anger with her. 'You could ruin me in a week!'

'As long as that!' she teased.

'I'm already ruined,' he groaned, his face buried in her hair. 'I don't want to do anything but spend the day in bed with you.'

She felt the same way, but they both had businesses to run, other responsibilities. 'We can be together later tonight,' she told him throatily.

'And every other night. They're all mine, Natalie,' he warned her. '*You're* all mine.'

Until someone else came along who attracted him more! But she had accepted that, she couldn't start wishing for what could never be now. The fact that last night she had told him she loved him wasn't mentioned by either of them, Natalie because she wished she hadn't burdened Adam with her feelings, and Adam, she felt sure, because he would rather not know about such emotions as love. Wanting and desiring were the emotions he understood, and he wanted no complications to that. And she couldn't blame him for that, she had known from the first what sort of man he was. It was too late now to decide it wasn't enough!

'Natalie?' he frowned at her silence.

She gave him a bright smile, determined to enjoy what time they did have together. 'I'm all yours,' she agreed.

He seemed to accept that. 'Do you mind about dinner tonight?'

'No,' she lied.

'I do!' he muttered.

'Adam!' She felt warmed by the honest way he expressed his desire for her.

He touched the glossy darkness of her hair. 'Five-thirty?'

'Yes,' and she kissed him.

Adam deepened the kiss, a fine sheen of perspiration covering his brow as he fought back the impulse to make love to her. 'I'll come home with you.'

'Yes.' She didn't miss his meaning at all. 'Adam,' she teased, 'are you sure you should go to work dressed like that?' She looked pointedly at the evening clothes he was still wearing.

'I don't intend to,' he smiled at her. 'I'm going to my apartment first. Although this problem will be solved as soon as you move in with me.'

Natalie swallowed hard. 'Move—in—with—you?' she repeated slowly.

Adam frowned. 'Don't you want to?'

'Well, I—I hadn't thought about it,' she replied honestly.

'Then do so. And fast,' he warned. 'I don't intend letting you go, Natalie.'

Her glow of happiness was with her all day, and if Dee was able to guess the reason for it she said nothing. But Adam telephoned her three times during the day, and more roses arrived from him late afternoon.

Natalie was waiting outside the building for him at twenty past five, eager to see him again, to be with him. They held hands all the way back to her flat, and the tension between them was almost too much to bear, their conversation was non-existent.

'Natalie!' Adam shuddered into her scented throat half an hour later, their clothes scattered in a pattern as they had progressed from the door to her bedroom, the trail of clothes easy to follow. 'I've never felt like this before,' he groaned. 'I can't stop thinking about you, seeing you——! It's madness of a kind, a delicious madness.'

Natalie felt the same way; she knew she belonged body and soul to this man, that this latest time in his arms had surpassed all that had gone before—and she hadn't believed that to be possible. 'Then we're both mad,' she held him to her, 'because I can't stop thinking about you either.'

They slept in each other's arms for some time. Adam was at last the first to stir. 'I hate to ruin a beautiful evening,' he murmured huskily, 'but Tracy's expecting us at eight, and it's seven-thirty now.'

'It is?' Natalie shot up into a sitting position, having lost all selfconsciousness of her nakedness in front of Adam long ago, as he had with her, and got out of the bed to go into the bathroom.

She hurriedly showered and dressed herself, knowing she looked good in the green silky knee-length dress as Adam's eyes darkened appreciatively. As it was, they were fifteen minutes late arriving at the Dillman house, an ultra-modern bungalow in the suburbs of London, Adam having to once again stop at his apartment first and change into the appropriate clothing.

But he had warned her, 'I don't intend doing that for much longer!'

The Dillmans lived in a quiet cul-de-sac. Their detached bungalow was right at the end, shielded from the road by several large trees. The Mercedes she knew to be Jason Dillman's was parked in the driveway, and a brown estate car parked in front of this.

'Tracy usually takes her dog with her everywhere,' Adam explained.

A housekeeper met them at the door, and if she was curious about Natalie accompanying Adam then she didn't show it as she took them into the lounge. Tracy came forward to greet them, looking very graceful and elegant in a white linen suit, her smile welcoming.

'Jason will join us in a moment, he's just on the telephone,' she explained with a smile.

'You have a charming home,' Natalie told her

sincerely, instantly liking the warm comfort of the green and cream lounge.

'Thank you,' Tracy accepted shyly.

They were all sitting down having a drink when Jason joined them, casually dressed in a brown shirt and trousers. Natalie could feel Adam's tension immediately the other man came into the room, sitting as close to him as she was, and she knew that if it weren't for love of his sister Adam would like to take Jason Dillman apart limb from limb.

It was a strained meal, with the two men barely on speaking terms. Tracy was once again the only one who seemed immune to the tension around her. When Tracy dismissed the housekeeper, making the coffee herself, Natalie decided to join her, the aged Golden Labrador padding along with them. It was a friendly dog called Sophy, and it obviously adored Tracy as much as she adored it.

'You and Adam are very close.' It was a statement from the other woman, not a question.

'Yes,' Natalie blushed.

Tracy nodded. 'I can see how happy you are together.'

'Your own happiness is equally obvious.'

The other woman arranged the cups on the tray. 'Is it?'

Natalie frowned. 'Isn't it?'

'Of course,' Tracy said lightly. 'What do you suppose the two men are doing?' she teased. 'Do you think they're at eash others throats yet?' Her eyes twinkled mischievously.

'Probably,' she laughed. 'Don't you mind?'

Tracy shrugged. 'I gave up worrying about it years ago. You aren't Adam's usual type at all, you know,' she said thoughtfully. 'And I'm not being bitchy.'

Natalie knew that; she doubted Tracy had ever been

bitchy in her life. Her own liking of the other girl had deepened tonight—and her dislike of Jason and her sister had grown. Tracy trusted her husband implicitly, and he took advantage of that trust to betray her.

'Does Adam have a type?' she mused.

'Oh, I don't mean he goes exclusively for blondes or redheads, or anything like that,' Tracy laughed. 'But his women are usually clinging, kittenish.'

'Like the Princess?' Natalie remembered the cloying redhead from the theatre.

'Maria?' Tracy's eyes widened. 'You've met her?'

'Not exactly,' she grimaced. 'But I saw her.'

Tracy giggled enchantingly, looking more beautiful than ever against the background of her own home. 'Then you know what I mean about clinging and kittenish. Maria makes an art of it. You're so different.'

Natalie smiled. 'I am?'

'You know you are. You're younger than most of them, for one thing, and you have an air of independence. You run your own business,' Tracy added as if to clarify the point.

Natalie had noticed how genuinely interested the other girl was in the fact that she had a career. Maybe Adam's ideas for his sister were good ones after all.

'Have you ever worked?' she asked softly.

Tracy flushed. 'No. I'd just left school when I met Jason, and since we've been married he hasn't encouraged me to go to work.'

No, she could imagine he hadn't. It wouldn't suit Jason Dillman at all to have his wife find a little independence by having a career.

'And there's really no need for it,' Tracy added almost defensively.

'I doubt if Adam needs to work either.'

'No,' the other woman flushed. 'But he isn't the type rich and idle playboys are made of.'

'And you're the type that rich and idle play*girls* are made of?' Natalie prompted.

'No,' Tracy sighed. 'But Jason's never liked the idea of my going out to work.'

'I see.' Natalie pursed her lips. 'Well, maybe you would like to come down to the agency some time and see how it works?' She made the suggestion as lightly as possible, seeing from the eager light in Tracy's eyes that the idea interested her enormously.

'When?' Tracy was filled with suppressed excitement.

Natalie shrugged. 'Any time. Whenever you're free.'

'I have hairdressing and dental appointments tomorrow, but how about Thursday?' Tracy said eargerly, showing just how empty she found her days.

'Thursday what, darling?' Jason strolled into the kitchen, looking at them both enquiringly, his arm going about his wife's shoulders. 'Adam and I were wondering what was keeping you both.'

Tracy looked almost guilty. 'Natalie was just inviting me to her agency on Thursday,' she informed him strongly.

Narrowed brown eyes were turned on Natalie, but she coolly withstood that gaze. 'Indeed?' he drawled.

Natalie nodded. 'I thought Tracy might like it.'

'I think it's a very good idea.' Adam joined them— much to Natalie's relief. 'You should find it interesting, Tracy,' his arm curved possessively about Natalie's waist.

'I thought so,' she nodded, eyeing Jason uncertainly.

'Well, if you insist on going . . .' Jason let his words hang in the air, his disapproval of the idea obvious.

Natalie found it difficult to keep quiet as she saw the battle going on within Tracy. The other girl was fully aware of her husband's disapproval, and yet the temptation to see the agency was proving too strong for her.

'I'll take you both out to lunch afterwards,' Adam offered firmly.

'Oh, that would be lovely,' his sister accepted eagerly.

Natalie noticed that Jason didn't echo the sentiment, that in fact he said little for the rest of the evening. Emotional blackmail, Natalie decided, but to Tracy's credit she didn't back down.

'That was a good idea of yours, darling.' Adam drove the Porsche with the minimum of effort, one of his hands momentarily leaving the steering-wheel to clasp hers. 'Jason didn't like it one bit,' he added with satisfaction.

'Thank goodness, Tracy did.'

'Only because she admires you, sweetheart,' he said with pride. 'As I do,' he added throatily.

'That isn't what Tracy said,' Natalie taunted.

Adam frowned. 'What do you mean? Tracy has never hurt anyone in her life!'

'And she hasn't now,' she assured him hastily. 'But she did tell me you usually like clinging women, women unlike me.'

'Did she now?' he mused.

'Mm,' she said primly. 'Kittenish women, like the Princess.'

'I told you she didn't like her,' he laughed softly.

'Neither do I,' Natalie laughed too.

He parked the car behind the MG outside her apartment building, then came round to open her car door for her. 'And you do cling, darling,' he told her as they entered the building together, his arm about her waist. 'At the right time,' he murmured against her earlobe.

'Adam!' she blushed.

He closed and locked the flat door behind them with obvious relief, shutting out the rest of the world to take her into his arms. 'I thought I'd never get you to myself!' he groaned, raining fevered kisses over her throat.

Natalie had felt the same way, and they lost no time in showing each other just how much they wanted to be alone together.

And they were alone, all night, and all the next day. When it came to morning Adam refused to let her get out of bed, and by the time they thought of such mundane things as time again it was after twelve and much too late to worry about going into their respective offices. Instead they made lunch together in Natalie's compact kitchen—compact compared to what Adam was used to, luxurious to her. After breakfast they dressed and went out to the park, walking hand in hand in the sunshine like two starry-eyed teenagers.

For Natalie their time together passed as if in a dream, a dream she wanted never to wake from.

But all too soon reality intruded. Adam had to leave early Thursday morning to get to a nine o'clock appointment he couldn't avoid.

'I have to go in myself today.' She held him down to her as he bent to kiss her as she still lay beneath the sheet, already fully dressed himself. 'Dee didn't sound too well when I spoke to her yesterday. Besides, I can hardly call Tracy and tell her I can't see her this morning because I want to stay in bed with her brother,' she grinned. 'I don't think she would understand.'

'She might,' Adam smiled, sitting beside her on the bed. 'But I don't think my client would. But I'll see you both for lunch, hmm?'

'I'll miss you.' Her arms clung about his neck.

'I'll miss you too,' he groaned. 'I'll make arrangements for us to be together all the time as soon as possible, shall I?'

Some of her happiness left her, and her gaze wavered from his. 'Let's leave it a while, shall we?'

'Why?' he rasped, frowning.

'It's all happened too soon, Adam. Let's not rush ourselves, Okay?'

For a moment he looked as if he might argue, then he nodded. 'Okay—for now. I'll approach you about it again at a more—vulnerable, moment.'

She laughed. 'That isn't fair!'

'I've never said I was fair,' he smiled, looking regretfully at his wrist-watch. 'But I am late. I hate to go, darling,' he stood up. 'I'll pick you and Tracy up at one o'clock.'

Natalie lay back in the bed once he had gone, feeling too happy to want to move. The last two days had been wonderful, marvellous—and she was missing Adam already. Physically she knew they were perfectly matched, knew that despite her inexperience she gave Adam as much pleasure as he gave her, that her mere touch caused a shudder of desire to course through his body. During the last thirty-six hours he hadn't been able to get enough of her, nor she of him, and even now she burned for his return.

When the doorbell rang as she chewed uninterestedly on a piece of toast she felt sure it was Adam, that he had been unable to leave her either!

The smile faded from her lips as she opened the door to her sister, and she held her wrap protectively in front of her as Judith's eyes widened derisively at her ruffled appearance, her face still bare of make-up, her hair in disarray. It was the way Adam liked her best, but Judith simply eyed her with mockery.

'Is it all right to come in?' her sister drawled.

'Of course.' Natalie flushed, relieved now that Adam had already left.

Judith swayed into the room, looking about her interestedly, sitting herself down on one of the bar stools in the kitchen. 'Any more coffee?' She eyed the pot.

Natalie poured her a cup, her hand shaking in her agitation. 'Sugar?'

'You know I never touch the stuff,' Judith watched her mockingly. 'You seem—nervous, Natalie.'

'Don't be silly.' She sat down, evading her sister's gaze. 'Why should I be nervous?'

'Could it have something to do with the fact that if I'd arrived ten minutes earlier I might have met Adam Thornton on the stairs?' Judith taunted.

The colour flooded and then ebbed from her cheeks, leaving her deathly white. 'Don't be silly, Judith——'

'Silly?' her sister derided. 'The only silly thing I seem to have done lately is think how pure and sweet my older sister is, and all this time you've been sleeping with Adam Thornton!'

'I——'

'The parents sang your praises all weekend, so much so I began to believe them,' Judith's mouth twisted. 'You see, none of us had any idea you were sleeping with Adam Thornton.' Her face hardened. 'I even argued with Jason when he told me you were.'

'Jason!' Natalie said disgustedly.

Judith's eyes flashed angrily. 'Don't be so high and mighty, Natalie. Especially as you're no better than we are now.'

'What's that supposed to mean?' she gasped.

'Jason told me exactly why you're sleeping with Adam,' her sister sneered. 'And I know you've been seeing him. I was talking to Jason on the telephone on Tuesday when you arrived for dinner with Adam.'

'At his own home!'

'Why not?' Judith dismissed.

'If you don't know I'm not going to tell you!' Tracy could have walked in on that telephone call at any time, and Judith didn't seem to give a damn!

'Oh, stop being so damned sanctimonious, Natalie!'

Her sister slammed her cup down on the breakfast bar. 'You're sleeping with a man simply to keep his business at your agency, and you——'

'*What did you say?*'

'Grow up, Natalie,' Judith sneered, standing up. 'You're sleeping with Adam Thornton so that he doesn't ruin your beloved agency. I know, you know it, and you can bet he knows it too!'

'Get out,' Natalie ordered shakily. 'Get out, Judith, and don't ever come back!'

'Oh, I'm going,' her sister drawled. 'I just wanted you to know you aren't deceiving anyone with your Goody-Two-Shoes act. We *all* know about you now.'

'*Get out!*' Natalie's voice was low and controlled.

She didn't even notice her sister leaving, pain such as she had never known before ripped through her brain and body. She didn't care what Judith thought, she didn't care what Jason Dillman thought either, but could Adam possibly believe *that* about her too . . .? Hell, she would want to die if he too believed she had gone to bed with him so that she didn't lose the Thornton business at her agency.

CHAPTER EIGHT

As Natalie sat there in numbed silence she knew he had no reason to think anything else. And hadn't he once questioned her practice not to query how the work came to her agency? Oh, he had been talking about Judith's involvement with Jason at the time, but she knew that the parallel could also be levelled at her now.

But she loved him, had told him of that love! And he hadn't acknowledged that love, had shown her only desire and need. Dear heaven, he *did* believe she had given herself to him because of her agency, because of Fantasy Girl!

Why shouldn't he? She had sacrificed her pride to help him with his sister when he had threatened her agency with ruin, why shouldn't he think her capable of sacrificing her body for the same reason?

The happiness she had known in his arms only an hour ago now seemed like ashes at her feet. The beauty and tenderness of their time together was all in her imagination; she was no more than just another willing woman to Adam, an ambitious willing woman at that. That was what hurt the most, the knowledge that Adam could believe she had done it only for ambition's sake.

How she ever dressed herself and drove to the office she never afterwards knew. She simply found herself unlocking the agency door, switching on the lights, putting on the coffee, doing all the things she usually did when she was first in in the morning.

When the harsh noise of the telephone rang out she dropped the steaming cup of hot black coffee she had just been adding sugar to, stepping over the shattered

fragments to pick up the receiver, watching uninterestedly as the coffee soaked into the black carpet,
more concerned with who could be calling her. If it
were Adam . . .!

'Natalie?'

She froze at the sound of the male voice, her fingers
clenching about the receiver. 'Yes?' Her voice was little
more than a choked whisper.

'Tom here. I——'

'Tom?' she realised with relief, as her tension began
to ebb.

'I didn't mean to startle you——'

'Oh, you didn't,' she assured him hurriedly. 'What is
it? Is there something wrong with Dee?'

'Couldn't I have just called to tell you how beautiful
you are?' he teased.

Natalie laughed at his flirting, friends with both of
the Jones's. 'Not if you want to remain in one piece,
no.'

'You've noticed my wife's violent tendencies too,
have you?'

'I hope Dee can't hear you, Tom,' Natalie chuckled.
This lighthearted teasing was exactly what she needed
to help make her feel normal again. If she ever did! Her
pride had taken a bitter blow today, her heart an even
harder one, and she didn't know yet whether she was
going to recover.

Or what she was going to do about Adam! She
couldn't continue this affair with him now that she
realised why he thought she had slept with him. It was
too painful, too—too degrading, and it made a
mockery of the love she felt for him.

'She can't,' Tom confirmed. 'I'm afraid she's in bed.
She wasn't feeling too good when she got home last
night, so I took her out for a meal, and now she's been
sick all night. What a waste of a good meal!'

'Now I definitely know Dee isn't listening! Has she had the doctor?'

'Hm, he thinks it's a tummy bug. I doubt if you'll see her again until Monday.'

Natalie had already guessed that. 'Give her my love, and tell her not to worry about a thing.'

'I will. Are you feeling better now?'

'Better . . .? Oh—oh yes,' she answered jerkily, blushing, although of course Tom couldn't see that. 'A lot better, thanks. I—I'd better go now.'

'Sure. See you.' He rang off cheerfully.

Natalie leant weakly against the desk, realising just how lost in her love for Adam she had become. She never took a day off work, she was always very conscious of her responsibility to the people who worked for her. But yesterday she had forgotten everything but Adam, and making love with him.

Work. That was what she needed now, work such as she had never known before. Only then would she perhaps be able to put Adam out of her mind.

Clearing up the mess from the spilt coffee wasn't exactly what she had in mind, but it was where she was going to have to make a start!

She was down on her knees scrubbing the carpet when the door opened and Tracy Dillman came in. Natalie closed her eyes momentarily, having completely forgotten since speaking to Judith this morning that the other girl was coming here today.

'So this is the glamour of a modelling agency!' Tracy grinned down at her.

Natalie sat back on her heels. 'We all have to start at the bottom,' her own humour was brittle; Tracy's likeness to Adam was too noticeable to cause her anything but pain.

'So I see,' Tracy giggled, looking very young and beautiful in the pure white dress that clung lovingly to her slender curves.

Natalie stood up, throwing away the debris from the broken cup. 'A slight accident, very clumsy of me. I'm afraid I'm on my own today, Tracy, and——' she broke off as the telephone rang.

For the next half an hour she seemed to have one telephone call after another. The telephone rang again every time she tried to talk to Tracy. At this rate it would be lunchtime before she had the chance to tell Tracy they would have to cancel this meeting until another day. Dee's absence was making it impossible for her to talk to Tracy today!

'Let me,' Tracy offered as the telephone rang once again, taking over the small switchboard with cool competence.

Natalie watched with wonder as Tracy dealt with a recalcitrant client as efficiently as Dee would have done, the person on the other end of the line seeming to be apologising to Tracy before they rang off.

'How did you do that?' she gasped.

'I took a secretarial course at school,' Tracy told her proudly. 'I watched you use the switchboard a couple of times, and it doesn't seem too complicated. The soothing manner was easy. I used to use it all the time when I lived with Adam. He seemed to have rejected women calling him day and night,' she grimaced.

Pain flickered across Natalie's set features. Soon she would just be another of Adam's 'rejected women'.

Contrition washed over the other girl's face. 'Hey, I'm sorry—I mean—Well, it was years ago. I'm sure that will never happen to you.'

Natalie's smile was bitter. 'I'm equally sure it will, in time.'

'No, I——'

'I haven't deluded myself about Adam and me,' Natalie lied coolly. 'When it ends I'll be ready for it.'

Because she was going to have to end it herself, if she wanted to regain her self-respect.

Tracy frowned. 'I thought you and Adam——'

She gave a dismissive laugh. 'We're both adults, Tracy.'

'But——' The telephone began ringing again. 'Let me,' Tracy offered once more. 'You go through to your office, I'll deal with this.'

'Do you type too?' Natalie asked dazedly.

'Do I!' Tracy smiled confidently.

'Like a job for the day?' she queried half teasingly, half seriously.

'I'd love it.' Tracy settled herself behind Dee's desk. 'Don't worry about a thing, it's all under control,' she grinned.

The ringing of the telephone seemed to be becoming insistent to Natalie's ears. 'I don't imagine our caller thinks so,' she derided.

Tracy winked at her, picking up the receiver to deal with this second caller as deftly as she had dealt with the last one. After the first few seconds Natalie left her to it. She felt sure Adam hadn't had this in mind when he asked her to help his sister, she doubted if a secretarial job was what he had in mind at all!

And Tracy was capable of more, had the confidence, away from Jason, to make a career for herself in any field she cared to.

A germ of an idea began to form in Natalie's mind, and grew to gigantic proportions. It was a fantastic idea, unbelievable, and yet the more she thought about it the more excited she became. She would discuss it with Adam when next she saw him. If he said no she would understand, but it was the perfect idea. *Tracy* would be perfect.

The morning passed quickly with the backlog of work from yesterday, with Tracy proving just how well she could type and smoothly handle impatient clients.

For Natalie the rushed morning was exactly what she needed to take her mind off Adam, and when Tracy put through a call to her mid-morning she had no thought of its being him. She began to tremble as soon as she heard his voice.

'How are you?' he asked huskily.

'Fine,' she answered briskly.

'How did Tracy's visit go?'

'Er—very well.'

'Did she enjoy it?'

'I think so,' she answered evasively, not too sure how he was going to react to being told his sister was acting as her secretary—if only for a day.

'You don't sound too sure?' he chided teasingly.

Natalie chewed on her bottom lip, not knowing how she was going to live without this man. 'Why don't you ask her yourself?' she suggested jerkily.

'I called her at home, but she isn't there. I think she must have gone shopping or something. That seems to be something you women——'

'Er—Adam,' she interrupted.

'Yes?'

'Tracy is still here.'

'She is?' His surprise could clearly be heard.

'Yes. You see——'

'I hope she isn't bothering you, she must have arrived very early. I thought maybe she would arrive half an hour before lunch or something. She must be enjoying herself,' he sounded pleased.

'She is,' Natalie grimaced.

'Can I talk to her?'

'You just did.'

'No, I—*That* was Tracy?' he sounded incredulous. 'That was Tracy who put my call through?' he wanted confirmation.

Natalie explained as quickly as she could how Tracy came to be acting as her secretary. Once she had finished she waited for his explosion.

'She sounded wonderful,' Adam said excitedly. 'Very cool and competent, very sure of herself.'

'She has reason to be.' Natalie felt more sure of *herself* now that Adam hadn't lost his temper. 'She's very good. But I'm afraid I won't be able to make lunch. I can't leave the office now.'

'No, I understand that. I'll pick you up from work tonight——'

'No! I mean—no,' she said more calmly. 'I have such a lot of work to do and I——'

'I need you, Natalie.'

She shivered pleasurably at the raw passion in his voice, unable to dampen the wild sensations quivering through her body. She *had* to see him, *be* with him, one more time at least.

'Natalie!'

'All right,' her voice was huskily soft. 'Pick me up from work. About six?'

'I'll be there. But I'll talk to Tracy now.'

'Adam, I have something I want to talk to you about, concerning Tracy. It's something important.'

'Can it wait until tonight?'

'Oh yes!'

'I'm not sure I can,' his voice was ragged. 'Darling, I miss you. I never knew a day could be so long.'

Natalie had never doubted Adam's desire for her, and she didn't now. She didn't doubt her own desire for him either, could feel her whole body tingling in anticipation of him. She needed him as badly as he needed her, for tonight at least.

'Darling, are you all right?' Adam sounded concerned. 'You don't seem to be with me.'

'Oh, I am,' she shook herself out of her self-torture. 'I'm very much with you.'

'I hope so. I certainly can't start without you,' he teased.

'Oh, Adam!' Natalie felt some of her tension leave her as she smiled. Tonight, just tonight, she promised herself.

She could hear Tracy laughing in the other office as she spoke to her brother on the telephone, and wished she could laugh with him as lightheartedly as that, that she hadn't had the truth thrown at her so cruelly.

Tracy came in a few minutes later, an excited flush to her cheeks, looking even more beautiful than ever. White was definitely her colour, seeming to give her an out-of-this-world delicacy, and all the time her eyes seemed to simmer with the same sensuality that her brother possessed in an even greater degree. It was this rare, even unique combination that had convinced Natalie that Tracy would make the perfect Fantasy Girl! Of course, she had no idea whether Adam would welcome such a career for his sister, but to her Tracy seemed perfect for the part. She intended putting that idea to Adam tonight.

'He thinks I'm doing very well,' Tracy told her breathlessly.

'You are,' she nodded. 'These letters are perfect.' She had been checking through the half a dozen letters Tracy had typed for her when Adam's call had come through.

Tracy flushed her pleasure. 'My typing is a little rusty, but I was picking up speed towards the end.'

'It's very good,' Natalie assured her, seeing how Tracy needed this boost to her confidence. 'I'm sorry about lunch.'

'That's all right,' the other girl dismissed. 'I'm having such fun here!'

Natalie grimaced. 'You wouldn't if you did it all the time.'

'Maybe I could come back and help out tomorrow if your secretary is still going to be out?' Tracy queried tentatively.

It would certainly be a help to her, but she wasn't the only one to consider. 'Maybe you should talk it over with Jason first,' she suggested softly.

A rebellious flush heightened the other girl's cheeks. 'It won't affect him, he's out at work all day anyway.'

'Nevertheless . . .'

'All right,' Tracy sighed, 'I'll call him now and tell him.'

Natalie had to smile at herself for the way Tracy intended 'talking it over' with Jason! It seemed Tracy could show some of Adam's determination when she wanted to.

From the bright glitter of tears in Tracy's eyes when she came back a few minutes later she didn't think the conversation with Jason had exactly gone smoothly. Nevertheless, Tracy informed her that she would be in to help her tomorrow too. Jason Dillman wouldn't be pleased by his wife's further rebellion at all.

She was still working at her desk, Tracy having left almost an hour ago, when Adam came quietly into the office at five-thirty. Natalie looked up at him with hungry eyes, eating up everything about him, the warm blue of his eyes, the dark thickness of his hair, his beautiful mouth and powerful body.

'I know I'm early,' he said huskily, his eyes devouring her in return, 'but I couldn't stay away any longer.'

She stood up as if in a dream, moving into the warm possession of his arms with a satisfied sigh. 'I'm glad,' she told him huskily.

He curved her body into his. 'Let's go home, hmm?'

'Yes,' she agreed gladly, wanting him to make love to her more than anything else in the world.

She was aware of a fierce desperation in her lovemaking that evening, a need to make herself actually a part of him, so that nothing and no one would ever be able to take him away from her again.

'Darling!' Adam shuddered beneath the sure caresses of her hands and lips, and lay back on the bed as she gave him exquisite pleasure.

He was nearing the end of his control, she could feel his body trembling with the sweet desire that would shortly send them both reaching for the brightness of the stars.

'Natalie!' He rolled over, pressing her into the bed beneath him, parting her lips with his, encouraging her to return the caress.

Natalie didn't need any encouragement, her caresses wild and abandoned as she felt the warm pleasure surging through her body, the excitement building up to such a pitch that when the hard thrust of his thighs melted into hers she felt herself dissolving in wave after wave of mindless ecstatic pleasure.

And Adam was far from finished with her yet, his body suddenly still on hers as he began to caress her breasts with his lips and tongue, sucking the nipples into his mouth as his hands curved her thighs into his and he began the slow movements of his muscled hips to bring her once again to the nerve-shattering fulfilment of her body with his.

He held her against his side in warm protectiveness as their breathing slowed and steadied to normal, their bodies still sensitised to the merest touch of the other.

'I can't believe this is happening.' His chest vibrated beneath her as he spoke. 'I'm thirty-nine, Natalie, and if I'm honest I'll admit to sleeping with more women than I care to think about.' His voice had hardened grimly.

'And yet this is the first time, every time with you, that I've known such a complete passion, a certainty that every caress, every kiss is *right*.'

Natalie felt that too, knew that a woman's first physical relationship could often be very disappointing, that often it took time and patience to reach the point of physical oneness they had achieved from the first.

Adam turned to look at her. '*Everything* is right with you.'

She blinked back the tears, cuddling into him, his skin firm and smooth beneath her touch, her body curved against his as she felt too disturbed to speak. Once again she didn't doubt his words, she knew that Adam would never lie to her, that he would always give her complete honesty. Just as he had never tarnished their relationship with false declarations of love.

'Tired?' he asked gently at her continued silence.

'A little,' she invented.

'Would you like me to cook dinner?'

'You can cook too?' she attempted to tease.

He grinned down at her, looking young and boyish. 'I'm very accomplished—as long as you don't mind eggs.'

She laughed, because she knew she had to. 'Strangely enough, I think eggs are all I have in the fridge.' She hadn't thought much about buying food lately.

'Thank goodness for that!' He got out of bed, pulling on his trousers once he had retrieved them from the lounge. 'I'll make you an omelette. I wonder if I'll ever have made love to you enough to take the time to put my suit on a hanger before I go to bed with you?' he mused ruefully.

Natalie leant on her elbow to watch him, the rose-red tips of her breasts jutting out temptingly. 'I don't know, will you?' she teased huskily.

'I doubt it,' he grimaced, standing up. 'Get yourself

dressed, woman, before I change my mind about cooking dinner and come back to bed.'

'I wouldn't mind,' she encouraged throatily.

'I know you wouldn't.' He touched her cheek with gentle tenderness. 'I love the way you enjoy me too, the way you don't make me beg for your body. So many women believe that there's a price for their body, but not you. You want to give, and so you do. But my reason for wanting to feed you is perfectly selfish—I want you to have the strength to make love with me for the rest of the night!' He ran a thumb-tip erotically over the hard tip of her breast.

She was wearing his white shirt when she joined him in the kitchen a short time later, loving the sensual feel of the silk material against her chin. Adam's eyes darkened as he looked at her, the shirt reaching to her thighs, her bare legs long and shapely.

'Suddenly I'm not hungry for food any more,' he murmured.

Natalie sat down on one of the bar stools, her bare legs under the breakfast bar now. 'I am,' she grinned at him impudently.

'Temptress!' he muttered.

'We have to be sensible and build our strength up for later,' she teased.

'So we do.' He put the plate of food in front of her, sitting at her side, his hand slowly caressing her thigh.

'Adam!' She squirmed as his caresses grew too intimate for her to even think of eating.

He held up both of his hands defensively. 'All right, I'll behave.'

Natalie made little attempt to eat the omelette and salad he had prepared, not being really hungry, although Adam obviously was, doing full justice to his own meal.

'And, as once promised, I'll have you for dessert!' He watched her with laughing blue eyes.

'I seem to remember already carrying out that promise!'

'So?'

'So,' she smiled her capitulation. 'Can we talk about Tracy first?' she sobered.

Adam grimaced. 'If we have to.'

'We do.'

He sighed. 'I knew I should have got that problem out of the way before I made love to you. But at the time I was going quietly insane.'

'And now?'

'Now I don't even want to think about Tracy.'

Neither did she, but she had to. 'I believe I've found a suitable job for her,' she told him.

He frowned. 'As your secretary? But I thought Dee——'

'No, not as my secretary,' she dismissed lightly. 'Although she's well qualified to be anyone's secretary if she wants to be. No, I have something more glamorous in mind.'

'Modelling?'

'Of a sort,' she nodded, watching for his reaction. There didn't seem to be one yet.

'She's had no training——'

'Tracy is ideal to be your Fantasy Girl, training or no training,' she told him breathlessly, watching the incredulity on his face, the rejection, then the frowning uncertainty. 'She's perfect, Adam, so naturally beautiful, a child and yet a sensuous woman. I've never seen anyone like her,' she finished excitedly, feeling some of the old adrenalin begin to flow at the thought of a success. And she had no doubt that Tracy would make a success of Fantasy Girl.

'Tracy . . .' Adam repeated disbelievingly.

'Yes. Think about her, Adam, not as your sister, but as a woman. I don't know if you want that sort of career for her, but as far as I'm concerned no one else could do it like she could.'

'Tracy,' he said more firmly, now, 'I have to admit I never gave her a thought as Fantasy Girl.'

'And now that you have?'

He nodded slowly. 'You could be right,' he murmured slowly.

'I know I am.'

Adam smiled at her. 'My efficient little business-woman! You may just have solved two problems in one go.'

Three. If she found him a Fantasy Girl she had nothing to do with, someone who wasn't connected to her agency, maybe he just might come to realise that she had given herself to him because she wanted to, and not for any reasons of ambition. It was a distant hope, but it *did* give her the hope that perhaps she wouldn't have to lose him after all.

Natalie took her own car to work the next morning, having a ten o'clock appointment that she had to drive to. The night in Adam's arms had passed all too quickly, and although they had slept little, she didn't feel tired, but revitalised by Adam's lovemaking. Their parting had been as reluctant as ever; Natalie had been unable to refuse when he said he would meet her at her flat tonight.

'Will you be able to manage on your own?' she asked Tracy concernedly before going to her appointment. 'I shouldn't be longer than an hour or so.'

'Don't hurry back on my account,' Tracy told her confidently. 'I'll be fine.'

'Dee's going to be so mad when she sees how competently you've coped in her absence,' Natalie grinned.

The other girl gave a rueful smile. 'I don't think she

has anything to worry about from me. I wouldn't want to cope at this pace all the time.'

'But you are enjoying it?'

Tracy nodded. 'Very much.'

'Thought any more about working?'

She shrugged. 'I often think about it. But Jason wouldn't like it.'

'It wouldn't have to inconvenience him. As you said,' Natalie forced lightness into her voice, when really she felt anger towards Jason Dillman for the restrictions he had put on his young wife's life. No wonder Adam was trying so forcefully to help his sister—he had been watching this emotional blackmail for seven years! Marriage should be give and take, and your partner in life deserved the politeness of being consulted about any decisions that may effect the marriage, but no man had the right to swallow up a woman's personality, to deny her the chance of a possible career for herself, not if she wanted one and there were no children to suffer at the hands of that career. 'He would be at work all day himself.'

Tracy chewed on her lower lip. 'I—I'm still thinking about it.'

'Well, think harder,' Natalie encouraged. 'You never know when the opportunity might come your way.'

'You're starting to sound like Adam!' the other girl grimaced.

'Really?' her tone was brittle.

'Yes. Natalie——'

'I really have to go,' Natalie looked pointedly at her wrist-watch, 'or I'll be late.'

'See you later,' Tracy nodded.

It was a long meeting, the discussion of one of her male models appearing in a series of aftershave advertisements. The man in question demanded a certain fee, the client refused to meet that fee, and so they were at impasse. It had gone on like that for over an hour, with Natalie knowing the client would give in eventually. Daniel Jerome was ideal for the advertisements they had in mind, being tall, dark and handsome, with the sort of body most other men could only dream of possessing. Daniel knew he was worth the fee, and fortunately so did the client, so a deal was finally agreed upon, then Natalie left for her office feeling as if she had been through the wringer—and back again.

It was with some relief that she arrived back at the agency, although the empty outer office worried her somewhat. She was late back for Tracy's twelve-thirty lunch, but she felt sure the other girl wouldn't have just gone out and left the office unattended like this.

As soon as she entered her own office she thought she knew the reason for Tracy's absence. Judith sat back in a chair blowing smoke up at the ceiling, a completely bored expression on her beautiful face.

Natalie slammed the door with a resounding thud. 'What are you doing here?'

Judith turned slowly to look at her. 'A nice way to talk to your little sister, darling! Mum and Dad would be so shocked,' she taunted.

'We aren't talking about Mum and Dad now,' Natalie snapped.

'No?'

'No!' She was becoming increasingly angry with Judith's behavior. 'Where's Tracy?' she demanded heatedly, worry creasing her brow.

'Gone,' Judith told her coolly.

The frowned deepened. 'Gone where?'

Her sister gave an uninterested shrug. 'Home. To a friend's. How should I know where she's gone?'

'But you do know, Judith.' She leant over the desk at her sister, her eyes bright with anger. 'What did you tell her? What did you *say* to make her leave so suddenly?'

'Natalie——'

'Tell me, damn you!'

'All right!' Judith ground out her own anger, standing up. 'I told her the truth. The truth!'

'Which was?' Natalie bit out.

'That Jason and I have been lovers for months now. That it's me he loves and not her.'

Natalie felt faint. 'You—told—her—that?'

'Yes!' her sister hissed. 'It's time she knew, time this charade came to an end. I want to be with Jason all the time, not just when he——'

'Where is Tracy now?' Natalie wasn't interested in what Judith wanted.

Judith shrugged, her mouth tight as she received no sympathy from her sister. 'She left.'

'Did she say where she was going?' Natalie frowned.

'No. Look, I don't want——'

'I'm not interested in what *you* want,' Natalie told Judith disgustedly. 'You're a selfish little bitch who undoubtedly deserves all the unhappiness that's going to come your way. But Tracy doesn't. If she's done anything stupid——'

'Stupid?' her sister echoed dazedly. 'You mean—suicide?'

'It is conceivable,' Natalie snapped. 'You did just tell her she's living with an unfaithful husband. And if anything has happened to Tracy Adam Thornton will be coming straight for your jugular.'

Not to mention hers! Where could Tracy be?

CHAPTER NINE

JUDITHS's dazed disbelief didn't last for long; her mouth turned back into a sneer. 'You're being hysterical, Natalie——'

'Then you obviously don't know Adam Thornton!'

'Not as well as you do, no!' Judith scorned, her eyes glowing with satisfaction as Natalie blushed involuntarily. 'And I wouldn't want to. He's a man who would demand your very soul. That intensity isn't for me. And I don't doubt Adam Thornton's reprisals, I meant you're being hysterical about Tracy Dillman. That young lady has more self-possession than you give her credit for—any of you.'

Natalie frowned. 'Does that mean Jason didn't want his wife told of your affair?'

'Not yet,' her sister shrugged. 'But I'm tired of waiting. And don't call me a selfish little bitch again,' she ordered in a bored voice. 'I know exactly what I am—and what I want.'

Natalie gave a snort of disgust. 'Well, you've got Jason now——'

'Yes,' Judith smiled, like a cat who had got the cream.

'Unless of course Tracy forgives him—yet again!'

Judith's smile wavered and dropped. 'Again . . .?'

'She's known of his affairs in the past,' Natalie exaggerated slightly, 'and she's always taken him back.'

Judith's mouth was tight as she went to the door. 'Not this time,' she bit out. 'I'll make sure of it.'

Natalie slumped down in a chair once her sister had left, frantic as to where Tracy had gone. After what

Judith had so callously told her she could have gone anywhere! What would she, Natalie, have done if she had been told of her husband's infidelity, of Adam's infidelity?

But he wasn't her husband, never would be her husband, only ever her lover, although in her heart she would always be his wife. She would never give herself to another man as long as she lived.

And now she would never give herself to Adam again. She allowed herself a few minutes to linger on her own suffering, knowing that Adam would never forgive her for causing his sister all this pain.

Poor Tracy, she had done nothing to deserve this, she had been sweetly loving to her husband. Once again Natalie felt the burning anger towards Judith for ending the other woman's blind happiness.

'Anything wrong, darling?'

Her head went up with a jerk, all colour paling from her face. 'Adam . . .!' she groaned hollowly.

Adam frowned his concern, coming to her side. 'What is it? What's wrong?'

Natalie wetted her lips nervously, sure that Adam would kill her here and now if she told him the truth, if he knew how badly Tracy had been hurt.

'What is it, darling?' He came down on his haunches beside her, the blue eyes full of concern.

Her hands framed his lovingly, memorising every feature so that she should never forget one arrogant line of his face, would always remember the distinguishing grey in the darkness of his hair, the sure blue eyes, the arrogant slash of a nose, sensually firm mouth and rigid jaw. It all made up the face of the man she loved. How she loved him! Tears filled her eyes and threatened to overspill.

Adam grasped her arms, shaking her roughly. 'For heaven's sake talk to me!' he rasped. 'What's happened?

Are you hurt?' He was avidly searching her body for signs of injury. 'Are you ill?'

'Hold me, Adam,' she fell into his arms. 'Just hold me!'

'Gladly,' he groaned, gathering her up against him, plundering her mouth with raw intensity. They were both shaking by the time they drew apart, and Adam's smile was rueful as he looked down at her. 'I've felt like part of me was missing all morning. Now I know which part.'

'You do?' Her voice was husky against the warmth of his chest.

'The best part,' he said tenderly.

Her smile was shaky. 'You missed me, then?'

'Always!' His arms were suddenly like steel bands. 'You're like a fire in my blood, the very beat of my heart. If you left me now I think I would die.'

It was the nearest he had ever come to saying he loved her, the nearest a man like Adam could admit to such a weakening emotion. But it wasn't love, and he had only said he couldn't bear for her to leave him 'now', who knew how he would feel a month from now, a week from now, when he had tired of the eager response of her body to his, and grew bored with looking at her face?

'Don't you believe me, Natalie?' he frowned as he saw the emotions of uncertainty flicker across her face.

'Yes.' She sounded breathless. 'I feel the same way, that's why I was a bit tearful a few minutes ago. But why are you here, Adam? I thought I wouldn't see you until this evening?' She desperately needed to find Tracy, to help her if she could, but she had to get away from Adam without alerting his suspicions. Already she had revealed too much of her distress to this astute man, although he seemed to be accepting her explanation about the tears.

His smile was teasing as he leant back against the desk, pulling her between his parted legs to link his hands together at the base of her spine. 'Didn't you want to see me?'

'Oh yes. I just——' she broke off as he began to chuckle. 'Swine!' she said ruefully.

Adam grinned down at her. 'I came to see Tracy, actually. Not that it isn't lovely to hold you like this too.'

'T-Tracy?' she repeated, instantly stiffening.

Adam seemed not to notice. 'Yes, where is she? Has she already gone to lunch?'

'Er—yes,' Natalie replied abruptly. 'She—she said something about going shopping.'

His smile was indulgent. 'I wouldn't be at all surprised. I was going to take her out to lunch and sound her out about Fantasy Girl. Never mind,' he shrugged, 'it will keep. I don't suppose you'd like to come out to lunch with me instead?'

'I can't,' she moved out of his arms. 'I can't leave the office.'

'Close up,' he encouraged. 'Just for the hour—or two,' he added temptingly.

Natalie wanted to agree, wanted to be with him, but her duty lay with Tracy now. She had to find the other girl, she just had to. 'I can't—darling,' she added placatingly as she saw him frown. 'Someone has to be here, and I—I have a lot of work to do.'

Adam bent low to kiss her, lingering on the trembling flesh that was her mouth. 'My dedicated little darling,' he said tenderly. 'I'll leave you to it, then.' He straightened. 'I wouldn't like you to accuse me of disrupting your work.'

He had already deeply disturbed her, and he knew it, leaving her with a throaty chuckle of satisfaction, the promise of further disturbances in his eyes for later tonight.

As soon as he had gone Natalie called Tracy's home, ascertaining from the housekeeper that Mrs Dillman was not at home. She had to believe the woman. That only left Jason Dillman. Would Tracy have gone to him and confronted him with the affair? It was what she would have done herself, and yet Jason wasn't in his offive when she called T.C.B.A. Out of sheer desperation she tried the house once again.

'Mrs Dillman just came in,' the housekeeper told her. 'But she isn't taking calls.'

Relief flooded through her as she asked the woman to tell Tracy she would be coming over to see her straight away. For the first time since the agency had opened she closed it during a working day. Dee or herself as usually in the office.

When she saw the silver Porsche parked outside the bungalow her heart sank. Adam had taken to driving himself the last few days when he had been staying with her, his chauffeur and the Rolls receiving an unexpected holiday, and she knew straight away that the Porsche could belong to no other man. But she had to go in, had to make sure Tracy was all right.

The housekeeper seemed very agitated when she showed her into the lounge, and Natalie was pacing the room when she heard the door slam with restrained force behind her.

She turned slowly, knowing what she would see. Gone was the gentle lover of an hour ago, and in his place was the coldly harsh man of their first meeting, a man with eyes of ice, a tight mouth and inflexible jaw.

'I——'

'Before you say anything,' Adam ground out with barely controlled fury, 'let me tell you that your part in this fills me with disgust!'

Natalie paled, her eyes huge and deeply blue-green in her chalk-white face. 'My part? But, Adam, please——'

'Please!' he echoed scornfully. '*Please*? You dare to plead with me after what you and your bitch of a sister have done to Tracy?'

She flinched at the steely dislike in his face. 'But I——'

'All the time I was at your office, holding you in my arms, *making love* to you,' he added grimly, 'you knew of the shock Tracy had received, that she wasn't shopping at all. And you lied to me, with your body and your eyes. As you have been lying to me from the beginning, as you *intended* lying to me. You knew I didn't want to go to bed with you until I had this situation with Tracy under control. But you couldn't wait to start our affair, could you? Oh no, you had to get me completely under your spell before Tracy and Jason split up.' His mouth twisted with dislike, his eyes glittering dangerously. 'You're no better than your sister after all!'

Natalie recoiled as if he had hit her. 'Adam, no——'

'What did you hope to achieve by sleeping with me? Did you hope that when your sister dropped this bombshell that I would be so besotted with your body that I wouldn't give a damn about the hurt you've caused Tracy?' His jaw was rigid.

Her head ached, her heart ached, her *body* ached. 'Adam——'

'Because I'm not,' he bit out, not letting her answer his accusations. 'I—enjoyed my time with you, revelled in it even, but no woman, *no* woman has ever, or will ever, mean more to me than the happiness of my sister. You lied and deceived me, and I'll not soon forget it,' he rasped coldly.

Her hands went out to him appealing. 'I had no idea Judith was going to talk to Tracy——'

'No?' Adam quirked a disbelieving eyebrow. 'From the little I've been able to ascertain from Tracy, your sister knew she was at the agency this morning. She went there determined to cause trouble. And she did.'

Natalie swallowed hard. 'I didn't tell her Tracy would be there!'

'No?'

'No! How could I have done?' she appealed. 'I was with you—all evening and all night.'

'Yes,' his mouth twisted. 'And it achieved nothing. You agreed to help me out with Tracy because of the reputation and success of your agency, and you *slept* with me for the same reason.'

'No!' she gasped, shaking her head, her worst fears being realised, the accusations all that she had expected.

'Yes,' Adam ground out once more. 'You have the same code as your sister. When all else fails, use your body!'

'I came to you a virgin!' Two bright spots of colour heightened her cheeks.

His mouth twisted. 'Which only goes to prove what price you put on that valued possession. You simply sold out to the highest bidder, my dear,' he drawled with contempt.

Natalie wasn't aware of moving, didn't know she had, until she saw the red welts of her fingers on the rigid cheek. Anger flared fiercely in dark blue eyes, and with a calculated coldness Adam lifted his hand and struck her hard across the face. Natalie closed her eyes at the moment of impact, feeling no pain, her whole body numb now. Adam's contempt was so much harder to bear than she had thought it would be.

She opened dull, lifeless eyes, seeing the pain flicker across Adam's hard face, knowing that even if he didn't love her he had liked and desired her. She had hurt him, or his pride, and his anger was all the fiercer because he had allowed her even that close to him. He had once admitted that only Tracy mattered in his life, and now he couldn't forgive Natalie for making him care about her too, if only for a few days.

Natalie held her head proudly erect. 'I have to see Tracy——'

'Never,' he told her grimly.

'I have to explain to her——'

'Any explaining to be done will be made by me,' he rasped.

She flushed. 'Then it will be biased.'

'You can bet you life it will be biased!' he rasped. 'I underestimated you, Natalie, believed the cool businesswoman and wanton lover were all of you. But I had it wrong, you're a cool lover too, cold and calculated.'

'How can you?' she choked. 'How can you even think such a thing?'

'I more than think it!'

'And you won't let me see Tracy?'

'No!'

The vicious denial made her tremble. 'At least tell me if she's all right!'

'Would you be?'

'No,' she admitted shakily.

'And neither is Tracy. For seven years she's put her love and trust in that swine,' his hands were clenched into fists at his sides, his anger now directed away from Natalie, 'and he allows one of his women enough confidence in their relationship to tell Tracy about their affair!'

'Judith . . .'

'Yes, your damned sister! Tracy is in her room now crying her heart out,' he revealed grimly. 'I should have known what was going to happen when Judith threatened me, but it was shortly after that I knew I had to have *you*.'

'You—you always *planned* to make love to me?' Natalie gasped.

His mouth twisted derisively. 'You didn't think it was all your idea, did you, Natalie?'

'I—I——'

'That desire for you made me underestimate your sister, and this last week I've been unable to think of anything but you.'

She knew what that admission cost him, and despite all the insults and accusations he had made in the last few minutes her expression softened with love for him. 'Adam darling——'

He shook off her hand. 'But I'm over that now. Tracy is the most important thing to me now——'

'She's important to me too! Oh, Adam, I didn't know what to do when Judith told me what she'd done,' she looked up at him pleadingly. 'And then you arrived, and——'

'You decided to bluff your way out of it,' he finished grimly. 'Tracy was waiting for me when I got back to the office, almost at collapsing point. But you can tell your sister she's lost. Tracy still wants the bastard, and this time I'll make sure he stays in line. He won't even breathe without my permission in future!'

Natalie wetted her lips nervously knowing that Adam meant what he said. Judith would be out of Jason's life from now on, as would any other woman except Tracy. 'And us?'

'Us?' he echoed in a hiss. 'There never was an "us", Natalie. I thought for a while there was, but any fool can delude themself when they want something badly enough. And I wanted you. I wanted that body of yours so badly I was willing to do anything to get it.'

'And now you've had it you don't want it any more,' she said bitterly.

'Exactly,' he bit out. 'Now I don't want it any more.'

'Then I might as well leave,' she said dully, feeling sick.

'Yes.'

'Give Tracy my love,' she looked at him with pained eyes. 'And tell her how sorry I am.'

'Are you?' he derided harshly.

'How can you doubt it?' she choked.

His mouth twisted. 'I can doubt a lot of things where you're concerned, mainly my sanity. But you had me blinded from the first.'

'So it's goodbye, then?' Her eyes were huge in her pale face.

'I don't think we ever said hello!'

No, they had been at loggerheads from the first word, and now like the adversaries they had been at the beginning they were parting with harsh words.

Adam moved quickly, pulling her roughly against him, brutalising her mouth in a kiss that told her more of his contempt for her than any words could ever do. His eyes glittered down at her as he pushed her away from him. 'Goodbye, Natalie. I hope I never see your beautiful face again!'

She flinched as if he had hit her again, stumbling to the door, not looking at him again, blinded by her tears. 'Give Tracy my message,' she choked breathlessly.

There was no answer from him, and the silence followed Natalie as she left the house.

She lived through that silence all afternoon and evening, her head seeming to be filled with a numbed void that allowed her to make all the right moves during an afternoon's work, to cook herself dinner, to even switch on the television set she rarely watched at the best of times. And during all that time she didn't allow herself to think of Adam once. She was afraid to, because once the ice cracked she wouldn't be able to stop the river of tears pounding inside her head from flowing and never stopping.

She still hadn't allowed herself to remember all the

bitterness that had passed between Adam and herself as she breakfasted the next morning, having slept restlessly, too weary to fight the waves of sleep that claimed her.

When the doorbell rang she instantly stiffened. Could it be Adam? If it was she was in for more abuse from him. And she couldn't take it, knew that her mask of composure would crack irrevocably if Adam began to berate her once again.

But if it was him he wasn't going to be put off; he was leaning on the doorbell now, the constant ringing jarring on the nerves after only a few seconds. And Natalie's nerves were too fragile at the moment to stand it more than a couple of minutes; she went to the door to wrench it open. The livid anger in the face of the man standing there filled her with apprehension.

'Where is she?' Jason demanded, pushing past her into the flat. 'Is she here?' he demanded as he walked through to the lounge, opening doors on his way as he searched the flat.

Natalie followed him, watching dazedly as he looked in every room. 'Tracy . . .?'

'No, not Tracy!' he snarled. 'Judith! Is she here?'

She shrugged. 'You can see she isn't.'

'Yes,' he sighed his impatience. 'Do you know where she is?'

'At home, I suppose.'

'I've tried there,' he bit out angrily. 'That was the first place I looked. She isn't there, hasn't been there all night by the look of it.'

Natalie frowned. 'How do you know that?'

'I have a key,' he derided.

'Oh,' she flushed. 'Well, she isn't here either.'

'As you said, I can see that,' Jason scorned. 'But you're her sister, you must know where she is.'

'You're her lover, do you know where she is?' she scorned.

His fingers bit painfully into her arms as he glared down at her. 'Don't get clever with me, Natalie! I don't have the time to waste. I've only managed to slip out of the house for a moment while Tracy sleeps and Adam went home to change his clothes. If I'm not back by the time Adam returns . . .!'

'He'll kill you,' she stated emotionlessly.

'If I'm lucky!' he grimaced. 'So, tell me where Judith is?'

'I have no idea,' she said truthfully. 'As far as I know she's at home.'

'I told you she isn't!'

'Then I don't know where she is,' Natalie snapped. 'But I do know she's unlikely to come here.'

'Been playing the prudish older sister again, have you?' he mocked.

'Get your hands off me,' she ordered coldly.

Jason released her so suddenly she almost fell, turning away to mutter. 'I knew I shouldn't have got involved with Judith, knew she would be trouble.'

'Then why did you?' Natalie snapped.

'Because I can't stay away from her!' he turned on her furiously. 'I'm obsessed with her!'

'And your wife?'

'I love her——'

'You have a funny way of showing it,' Natalie scorned, wondering how this man ever justified his actions to himself, let alone anyone else.

'Mind your own damned business——'

'It *is* my business,' she flared. 'You and Judith made it so!'

'And Adam?' he derided tauntingly. 'Did he make it your business too?'

She flushed. 'My relationship with Adam has nothing to do with you.'

'I doubt it has much to do with you either now,' Jason taunted. 'Adam's tongue can cut like a knife when he wants it to.'

'You should know!'

'Yes. And so do you now.'

Her mouth tightened. 'Why do you want to see Judith?'

'Why do you think?'

Natalie shook her head. 'I have no idea.'

His face darkened. 'The little fool nearly ruined everything for me,' he rasped, 'telling Tracy like that!'

'You're going to stay with Tracy, then?'

'Unless Judith can keep me in the comfort to which I've become accustomed,' he drawled. 'And she can't.'

Natalie's heart went out to Tracy Dillman, but she could also spare a little pity for her sister. Jason Dillman was utterly selfish, had no intention of leaving his wife if it also meant he lost his lifestyle. She had no idea how one woman could love a man like that, let alone two of them.

Jason smiled, a smile without any real humour. 'Don't look so shocked, Natalie. You're no better than me in your own sweet way. Poor Adam,' he mocked. 'What a blow to his ego to find you were just another opportunist. How he must hate you for that!'

She had paled more and more with each successive word, wanting to knock the smile off this man's face. But she wouldn't soil her hands with him, turning her back on him. 'Would you please leave?' she said tightly.

'Don't worry, I'm going. I've been out long enough already. But if you should see Judith——'

'I'll tell her you're looking for her,' she nodded distantly.

'You can tell her more than that,' he rasped. 'Tell her to stay away from me in future, that it's over between us.'

Natalie gave him a look of disgust. 'I have no intention of doing your dirty work for you.'

'Okay, don't bother,' he snapped. 'I'll tell Judith myself!' and he slammed out of the flat.

Where could her sister be? It wasn't like her to just go off like this without a word to anyone. She had certainly made Jason angry with her disappearing act.

When her doorbell rang again an hour later she knew it had to be Judith—at least, she hoped it was. This situation was bad enough already without Judith leaving her in the lurch.

It was Judith, a still confident Judith as she strolled into the lounge. 'You look terrible, Natalie,' she drawled critically. 'You aren't letting this get to you, are you?'

'This . . .?' Natalie repeated, too dazed to take in what her sister was saying.

'This business with Tracy——'

'This "business" with Tracy happens to be your affair with her husband,' Natalie snapped, incredulous at her sister's calm. 'Or have you forgotten that?'

'Of course not, darling,' Judith sprawled herself in a chair. 'It's been on my mind a lot.'

'So it ought to be——'

'That's why I stayed with friends last night,' she drawled, smoothing her hair delicately. 'To give Jason time to calm down. He would have been very angry with me yesterday for ending this farce.'

'I have news for you,' Natalie said dryly. 'He's still very angry.'

'How do you know?' her sister demanded sharply. 'Have you seen him?'

'He's been here,' she confirmed, not surprised that her sister hadn't broken her record and shown a little concern for Tracy Dillman. Jason and Judith were two of a kind.

'When?' Judith gasped.

'Not long ago, actually.'

'And you say he was still angry?' she chewed thoughtfully on her lower lip.

'That's an understatement!'

'Thank goodness I missed him,' Judith sighed, plucking absently at her silky dress.

'You haven't won, you know, Judith,' Natalie told her softly.

Hard blue eyes narrowed questioningly. 'What do you mean?'

'He's going to stay with his wife.'

'No!' Judith denied heatedly, and stood up, her hands clenched at her sides.

'Yes.'

Judith's eyes glittered determinedly. 'We'll see about that!'

'He told me himself,' Natalie sighed.

Her sister nodded. 'Maybe he did. Jason doesn't know what's good for him.'

'And you do, I suppose?' Natalie's brows rose mockingly.

'Oh yes,' Judith gave a hard smile. 'I know exactly what's good for him—me,' she said emphatically.

With Judith's conceit she was probably right! But only Judith seemed to think so. Adam would certainly make sure his brother-in-law would never stray again.

'Judith,' she coaxed softly, 'let him go. He isn't free, he never will be. Adam is a powerful man——'

'Ah yes, your lover,' her sister scorned.

'Not any more,' Natalie muttered.

'Finally couldn't stomach your connection to me, hmm?' Judith mused. 'What a stupid man!'

'Judith——'

'Oh no!' her sister's eyes widened at the agony in Natalie's pale face. 'You *love* the man!'

She flushed at the derision. 'And why shouldn't I? If you can love someone as obnoxious as Jason Dillman surely I can love a man as honest as Adam.'

'Why not?' her sister shrugged uninterestedly. 'And Adam Thornton's power doesn't frighten me. Jason will never stand for his interference in his life, he never has. And I'll still be waiting when he walks out.'

'I thought it was because you were tired of waiting that you engineered this situation?' Natalie reminded bitterly.

Judith's mouth twisted. 'Don't worry, it won't be for much longer.'

She couldn't doubt her sister's confidence, or the conviction of her words. Judith did truly love Jason Dillman, even knowing all his faults. There was certainly no happy ending to this situation.

'The parents know, by the way,' Judith added carelessly. 'I rang them and told them last night.'

'Oh, no...!' Natalie groaned.

'Yes,' her sister smiled.

She swallowed hard. 'What—what did they say?'

'They were wonderful, very understanding. Cheer up, Natalie, maybe when Adam calms down he'll realise what a fool he's been.'

Natalie slumped into a chair once Judith had gone, marvelling at the sheer nerve of her sister. Although she doubted Judith had told their parents the whole truth about——

'Can I come in?' requested a subdued voice. 'The door was open and——'

'Tracy!' she looked up to exclaim, her breath catching in her throat at the change in the other woman since yesterday morning. Always fragilely beautiful, Tracy now looked like porcelain, her cheeks ashen, her eyes huge in her pale face. Natalie suddenly remembered. 'Judith ...!'

'I heard the two of you talking and kept out of the way until she left,' Tracy revealed huskily.

She swallowed huskily. 'You—heard us?'

'Yes,' Tracy nodded. 'I heard everything that was said about Jason.'

Natalie wetted her lips nervously, and stood up. 'Judith doesn't mean it. She won't cause any more trouble. And Jason will never leave you,' she assued her.

'Won't he?'

'No,' she said with certainty, sure that Adam would control that situation from now on.

'I hope you're wrong, Natalie,' the other woman choked. 'I sincerely hope you're wrong.'

Natalie blinked. 'I—You do?'

'Yes,' Tracy's voice was harsh. 'Because if I have to live with Jason another day I think I'll truly go mad!'

CHAPTER TEN

NATALIE paled, frowning deeply. 'Tracy . . .?'

'Can I sit down?' the other woman swayed where she stood.

'Of course.' She led her to a chair, noticing how badly Tracy was trembling as she sat down. 'I'll just close the door.' She moved to do so, giving the other woman time to compose herself, although her own thoughts were spinning.

Tracy looked up as Natalie returned, a firm determination in the depths of her blue eyes, looking more ethereal than ever, her beauty achingly tragic. 'I meant it, Natalie,' she said firmly. 'I can't live with Jason any more.'

Natalie clasped her hands in front of her, not knowing what to say to help Tracy.

'Adam thinks I should stay with him——'

'*Adam* does?' she frowned, sure that couldn't be right. If Adam had his way Jason wouldn't even be in the same country as Tracy.

'Yes,' the other girl said heavily. 'I had to wait until he left the house before I could get away.'

Poor Adam, the whole of the Dillman family seemed to have done an exodus on him the moment he turned his back. 'I'm sure you're wrong about Adam,' she said huskily. 'He only wants you to be happy.'

'With Jason? How could any woman be happy with him? He's cruel and selfish, and I—I hate him!' Tracy finished chokingly, her face buried in her hands. 'I tried, Natalie, I tried so hard! But I can't stand it any more. If Adam forces me to go back to him I think I'll die!'

'He won't do that,' Natalie denied with certainty. 'Not if you really don't want to go back. He only wants for you what you want, Tracy.'

'But yesterday——' she shook her head. 'He said he would *make* Jason stay with me.'

'Only because he thinks that's what you want!'

Tracy shuddered. 'Not again. Not ever again.'

Natalie sat on the carpeted floor at the other woman's feet. 'Tell me about it, Tracy,' she encouraged softly. '*Talk* to me.' She felt sure there was something Tracy had never done since she had first married Jason Dillman seven years ago, and that was to tell someone about her marriage.

Tracy's eyes became glassy, her thoughts inwards. 'I was so happy at first, in love with love, I suppose. I so enjoyed being a wife. But Jason didn't enjoy being a husband,' her voice hardened to bitterness. 'From the first he hated the restrictions of marriage. But I didn't know that then, I was so caught up in my own little world of being a wife that I didn't realise Jason didn't feel the same way. We'd only been married six months when he had his first affair.'

'First . . .?' Natalie echoed hollowly, remembering that Adam had told her Tracy had never known about the other affairs.

'Jason has always had other women,' Tracy told her. 'After the first one I took stock of my life, took half, if not more, of the blame for Jason's wandering, realised that I had been so intent on being Mrs Jason Dillman that I'd forgotten *Mr* Jason Dillman. I did everything I could to make up for that, to show him how much I loved and needed him.' She shuddered. 'Three months later he had another woman. That affair lasted two months. The next one six months. The next one four. The next one——'

'No more, Tracy,' Natalie clasped her hand comfortingly, able to feel the other girl's pain now.

Tracy swallowed hard. 'I know the duration of all of them, during the whole of the seven years. A wife has a way of knowing such things,' she revealed dully. 'This last time—I'd just never knowingly met one before—and I say knowingly, because any number of our so-called friends could have been his latest woman.'

'My sister is a bitch!'

Tracy gave a bitter smile. 'Don't blame her, Jason can be very charming when he wants to be.'

'Why didn't you leave him years ago?' Natalie asked the question that had been bothering her the whole of the time Tracy told of the tragedy of her marriage.

The other woman sighed, shrugging, 'I had defied Adam to marry Jason. Adam has always looked after me, ever since our parents died whe I was sixteen he's protected me. I fell in love with Jason when I was on holiday, little realising that half of my attraction for him, *most* of my attraction to him, was my money.'

'I think you underestimate your own beauty——'

'No,' Tracy shook her head. 'Jason has expensive tastes, and as my husband he's been able to realise them all.'

'You still haven't explained why you didn't leave him,' Natalie prompted softly.

'Adam.'

'Adam?'

'I couldn't let him down,' Tracy revealed huskily. 'By marrying Jason at all I had let him down, if I'd also left him I would have hurt Adam unbearably.'

'No——'

'Yes,' the other woman sighed.

Natalie shook her head, thinking of the irony of the situation. How could this brother and sister, who loved and cared for each other so much, be so wrong about each other's true feelings?

'So I made the best of my marriage,' Tracy continued

softly,' tried to be the retiring obedient wife Jason seemed to want. And sometimes it wasn't easy,' she revealed fiercely. 'Sometimes it was almost impossible!'

'No one would have guessed how you felt.'

'No one was supposed to!'

'Especially Adam.'

'Especially Adam,' Tracy nodded. 'But I can't go on any longer. I heard what your sister said about you and Adam, and I'm sorry things are over between you, but could I please stay here with you until I decide what I'm going to do with the rest of my life?'

Natalie didn't hesitate. 'I'm glad you came to me,' she squeezed the other girl's hand. 'I—I tried to see you last night.'

'Adam told me,' Tracy said softly. 'That was what made me wonder if you wouldn't help me, just for a few days. I'm so tired,' she put a hand up to her temple as if it ached. 'So very tired!'

'Then sleep,' Natalie stood up decisively. 'Go into my bedroom and sleep. We can talk again when you wake up, if you want to.'

'Thank you!' Tracy grasped her hand gratefully. 'I couldn't think who else to turn to, and you'd already been so kind to me.'

'I'm very glad you came to me,' Natalie smiled gently. 'Now I'll show you the bedroom and then you can rest. It will be easier to think when you aren't so tired.' She led the way to her bedroom, turning back the covers. 'Sleep as long as you want to,' she invited. 'No one will disturb you.'

'I need this so badly.' Tracy sank down wearily on to the bed, slipping off her shoes, her eyes closing, and almost immediately she was asleep.

Natalie stood for a moment looking at her, at the vulnerable droop of her mouth, the frown that marred her brow even in her sleep. Poor Tracy, what unhappiness she had already known in her young life! But there was no reason why her suffering should continue, no reason why she should be apart from her brother. Adam loved Tracy, and he would do anything for her, even see her through the broken remains of her marriage.

As soon as Natalie got back to the lounge she put a call through to Adam's apartment, relieved when it was his own terse voice that recited the number. 'Could you come over here, Adam——'

'Natalie?' he growled impatiently.

'Yes.'

'I don't have the time to talk to you now, Natalie,' he dismissed curtly. 'And I certainly can't come to your flat. Tracy's housekeeper has just called me—she's disappeared.'

'She's here, Adam,' she told him quietly, hearing the raw concern in his voice.

'*There?*' he thundered disbelievingly.

'Yes. You see——' The line had gone dead.

Natalie was waiting for him when the doorbell rang a few minutes later; she let him in without a word being spoken, but knowing he followed her into the lounge, as conscious as ever of his presence.

She studied him as he looked about him with ill-concealed impatience. He looked haggard, more weary even than Tracy, and Natalie's hands ached to smooth the lines from his brow, to soothe the harshness from his face. But she knew he wouldn't welcome any show of love or tenderness from her, that his rejection of her had been complete.

His eyes finally narrowed on her, icy blue, clearly showing his contempt for her. 'You said Tracy was here.' It was an accusation.

'She is,' her voice was husky. 'She's sleeping—No, Adam,' she ordered as he would have immediately gone into her bedroom—reminding her all too vividly how intimately he knew that room, and her. 'Don't disturb her,' she instructed abruptly. 'What she needs now is sleep.'

'Here?'

She flushed at the scorn in his voice. 'She came here because she needed to talk to someone——'

'You!' His mouth twisted.

'Yes—*me*!' Her eyes flashed. 'I'm sorry if it's meant you've had to "see my beautiful face again",' she bitterly remembered his parting words of the night before. 'But your sister blames me for nothing. In fact she——'

'Yes?' he prompted at her abruptly bitten off words.

Natalie avoided his gaze. 'I think Tracy should tell you herself.'

'Tell me what?' His eyes were narrowed.

'It isn't for me——'

'Tell me, Natalie!' He swung her round, hurting her, deliberately so.

She met his gaze unflinchingly. 'I can't.'

'Why the hell not?'

'Because if Tracy wants to talk to you, she will. But if she does——' she paused, wetting her lips nervously. 'Listen to her, Adam.'

'What's that supposed to mean?' he rasped. 'I always listen to Tracy. She——'

Natalie sighed. 'Don't be so sensitive, Adam! I wasn't being critical. I know how much you love your sister, and I know you only want to help her.'

'But?'

She shrugged. 'Somehow the two of you have your wires crossed.'

'How?'

'You'll have to wait until Tracy wakes up and discuss it with her.'

'When will that be?' he asked wearily.

'I have no idea. But by the look of her, several hours.'

'Damn!' He sank down into an armchair, running a hand over his furrowed brow.

'You look tired yourself.' Natalie stood in front of him. 'The bedroom is occupied, but I can offer you that chair if you'd like to sleep.'

He looked up at her, frowning. 'Why are you doing this?'

She gave a rueful smile. 'Being a hotel for your family?'

'Yes.'

'I was a Girl Guide when I was younger,' she derided. 'Maybe that accounts for my helpful streak. Or maybe I'm just a glutton for punishment,' she shrugged.

'You have to be!'

Her mouth tightened. 'Do you want the chair or not?'

Adam's expression relaxed somewhat. 'I'd prefer the sofa,' he admitted ruefully.

'Be my guest,' she invited abruptly.

He was much too long for her sofa, his feet hung over the end, and he shifted about uncomfortably for several minutes. 'Damn,' he muttered, standing up to remove his jacket, putting a couple of cushions on the back of the sofa before stretching out again, his blue shirt taut across his broad back.

'Better?' Natalie asked huskily.

'Much,' he mumbled. 'But I never noticed how lumpy this sofa was the last time I lay on it. Maybe because that time you were with me.' An unbidden warmth deepened the colour of his eyes. 'Care to join me now?'

She swallowed hard, but sat down in the chair opposite him, her legs drawn up beneath her. 'Not this time,' she shook her head.

'I had a feeling that would be your answer.' He closed his eyes.

Several minutes later Natalie knew by the deep, even tenor of his breathing that he was fast asleep. She stood up to get him a blanket from the cupboard, laying it gently over his still form.

Silence reigned in the flat as the minutes ticked away, and even Natalie dozed in her chair, although she was aware of every noise, and she woke with a start as Adam turned over with a groan, his lean length very uncomfortable on the short sofa.

After that Natalie stayed awake, memorising each hard plane of his face and body. She doubted he would give her the opportunity of seeing him this vulnerable again.

Finally, about an hour later, he began to wake up, groaning tiredly, stretching his arms and legs after being in that cramped position while he slept. He turned to look at her with alert eyes. 'Have I been asleep long?'

'Just over an hour.' She swung her legs to the floor. 'Like a cup of coffee?'

Adam sat up, smoothing his ruffled hair back from his face. 'If you wouldn't mind putting a tot of whisky in it?'

'Not at all,' she smiled. 'Have you eaten today?'

'Not that I can remember,' he grimaced. 'Don't be too kind, Natalie, or I'll start to feel a bastard.'

Her mouth tightened. 'Meaning you don't already?' she said hardly, and went through to the kitchen.

She was shaking by the time she reached the sanctuary of the other room, leaning weakly against the cupboard, her own lack of sleep and food taking its toll on her.

But she was in control of herself by the time she took in Adam's coffee, carefully avoiding all contact with him before going back to prepare him some late lunch. She hadn't known when she told him Tracy was here that she would have to spend this time alone with him, and the strain was beginning to tell on her.

'Natalie . . .!'

She spun round to find he had followed her, dangerously close in the confines of the small kitchen. 'I—I was just going to cook you some lunch.' She moved away from him jerkily.

'That can wait.' He shook his head, his eyes intense. 'I think we need to talk.'

'We already have,' she recalled bitterly.

'*I* have,' he corrected huskily. 'I didn't allow you to say anything. I think I may have been wrong about you.'

'Only *think*?' she derided.

'Hell, Natalie, I don't know what to think any more. You——'

'Adam!'

They both turned at the sound of that breathless gasp. Tracy was standing pale-faced in the doorway. After an accusing look in Natalie's direction she ran back to the bedroom to get her shoes—intent on making her escape from both of them.

'Go to her,' Natalie encouraged Adam. 'Make her talk to you.'

'Yes.' He grasped her arms, his eyes intent. 'And later, can I talk to you?'

'Do you want to?' She sounded weary.

'Yes,' he told her simply.

She flushed. 'Maybe when you've spoken to Tracy,' she nodded.

He turned abruptly and followed his sister, closing the bedroom door behind him for greater privacy. Natalie busied herself in the kitchen, not wanting to inadvertently overhear the conversation between brother and sister.

Her own conversation with Adam she refused to even

think about, not wating to raise her hopes only to have them dashed once they did actually talk. She doubted that they could ever go back to their former relationship—even if they wanted to. Too much had happened for that.

Adam was white-faced when he came into the kitchen half an hour later, and Natalie wordlessly handed him a cup of hot coffee, the first cold remains thrown away.

He took a large swallow, not even seeming to notice the liberal amount of whisky she had put in it. 'I had no idea,' he muttered heavily at last.

She put a consoling hand on his arm, feeling his bewilderment. 'You weren't supposed to—no one was.'

He sat down heavily on one of the bar stools, his face in his hands. 'I can't believe it. Seven years,' he groaned. 'Seven years of her beautiful life wasted!' His eyes were tortured as he looked up at Natalie. 'Well, she's lived with that mistake long enough. She won't be seeing Jason again.'

'She could stay here——'

'Thank you, Natalie,' he said with genuine feeling. 'But I think it will be better if I get Tracy away from London for a while. Jason isn't likely to give up without a fight, and Tracy has suffered enough at his hands already. I'm going to drive her to an aunt's of ours out of town. When I get back I'd like to talk to you.' He stood up, moving to hold her in his arms, trembling against her. 'I——'

'Adam?' Tracy called from the lounge. 'Oh—er—Sorry.' She stood awkwardly in the doorway.

'That's all right.' Natalie moved out of Adam's arms, going to the other woman, a palely composed woman now, with a quiet confidence. 'Forgive me?' she asked huskily.

'I'm very grateful!' Tracy hugged her, smiling as she moved back. 'And I'm sure Adam is too,' she looked indulgently at her brother.

Natalie's smile remained fixed on her face as she watched the departure of the brother and sister. It was only when they had gone that her mask slipped. Gratitude! From the start their relationship had been based on all the wrong emotions—need, desire, want, hate, and now finally gratitude. She didn't want Adam's gratitude, she wanted his *love*. And she could no longer accept anything less than being his wife.

It was almost ten o'clock when the ringing of the doorbell told her of his return. She had almost given up any idea of him coming back tonight.

He had been home and changed into denims and a brown fitted shirt, his hair freshly washed and gleaming, his jaw newly shaved. Natalie felt very untidy next to him, her own denims and shirt creased, her face free of make-up, her hair in need of combing.

'How is Tracy?' she asked once they were seated opposite each other in the lounge.

'Shattered,' he sighed. 'But strangely serene. It will take her a long time to get over her marriage to Jason, but I think she will eventually.'

'I'm sure of it,' Natalie nodded, confident in the other girl's strength of character.

'I really thought she loved him. you know. I didn't see how she could, but I thought she did.'

'I know that.'

'So does she, thank God,' he rasped. 'I would never have kept them together otherwise. I've seen Jason,' he added heavily.

'And?'

'It's shaken him completely. He was sure Tracy loved him too.' His mouth twisted. 'But not any more. I don't know what it makes me, but I took great pleasure in telling him exactly how Tracy feels about him.'

'It makes you her brother,' Natalie said softly. 'I

don't know how you've restrained yourself all these years.'

'Strangely enough I felt sorry for him in the end.' He gave a rueful shrug.

'You have no need,' she shook her head. 'Do you think he'll go to Judith now?' She knew it was what her sister was waiting—hoping for.

'He could do,' Adam shrugged. 'Would you mind? In a way I think they could be suited for each other.'

'Deserve each other, you mean!' Natalie sighed.

'And you and I?' he said softly, sitting forward in the chair. 'Do we deserve each other too?'

She had stiffened as soon as he verbally coupled the two of them together. They weren't a couple, never had been; they had only ever shared a desire that in the end neither of them had been able to deny.

'I don't think so.' She turned away.

'Don't do that!' He came down on the carpeted floor in front of her. 'Don't ever turn away from me again, Natalie,' he pleaded.

She hardened her heart. 'Why not? You turned away from me.'

'Oh, hell!' he groaned, closing his eyes, a bright sheen to their dark blue depths as he looked at her once again. 'Yes, I turned away,' he admitted raggedly. 'Because for the first time in my life I was in love—and I didn't know how to handle it. No woman had ever given herself to me like you do. I didn't know how to trust you or accept the love for what it was. When this business with Tracy blew up in my face I felt betrayed by you.'

Natalie's breathing was so shallow she barely breathed at all. 'In love ...?' Only that seemed to matter at the moment.

'Yes,' he admitted self-derisively. 'I love you so much I can't think straight most of the time.'

'But you—you never said . . .'

'No,' he agreed heavily. 'You see, I could never be sure of you. When I made love to you and found I was the first, I thought that must mean you felt something special for me. But I couldn't be sure whether the love you said you felt for me afterwards——'

'So you did hear that!' she blushed.

'Yes,' he said softly. 'But I didn't know if you genuinely meant you loved *me* or whether it was because we'd felt such pleasure together when we made love. You never said it again.'

'And you never said it once!'

'I'm saying it now,' he told her quietly. 'I love you so much, Natalie. I can't go on without you. I—I've never been in love before, and I don't exactly trust the emotion——'

'As you don't trust me,' she reminded him bitterly.

Adam's shoulders were slumped as he stood up to leave. 'I've hurt you too much, haven't I?' he muttered.

'Mistrusted me too much,' she corrected huskily. 'How can you love someone and yet not believe a word they tell you?'

'I don't know,' he said dully, lines etched into his face. 'But I do love you. I need you too.'

'You've already had me, Adam,' she said numbly. 'You said you didn't want me any more.'

'I said that in anger——'

'But you still said it!'

His mouth twisted. 'I can remember some things you've said to me that you've later regretted. I've always believed it's never too late to tell someone you're sorry. And I am sorry, Natalie. Why won't you believe me?'

She did believe him, knew that he could never humble himself in this way if his feelings weren't genuine. But loving her still wasn't enough. She was greedy, she wanted all of him.

Adam took her silence as damning, bracing his shoulders determinedly. 'I may as well leave, then,' he murmured softly.

'Yes,' she sighed, wondering how she could bear to let him go.

'I would have been a good husband to you, Natalie,' still he delayed leaving. 'You're the only woman I've ever loved. But if I can't have you, I don't want anyone.'

Natalie was still stunned by the word she had thought Adam would ever use in a relationship. Husband . . . And he wanted *her* to be his wife!

'I love you,' he told her throatily. 'I really love you.' And he turned to leave.

'Adam!' She was out of the chair and running towards him. 'Did you just say husband?'

He frowned down at her. 'Yes.'

'But to be a husband you have to get married.'

He nodded. 'That is the usual practice, yes.'

'And to be *my* husband, you have to marry *me*,' she persisted impatiently.

'I'd like nothing better.'

'But neither would I!'

The wariness began to leave him, his expression lightened. 'Are you asking me to marry you, Miss Faulkner?'

'No, I——'

'Temper, temper!' he began to chuckle as his tension was released, his arms about her as he held her struggling body hard against him. 'All right, Natalie, I'll ask you. Will you marry me?' He was suddenly serious.

'Yes!' She threw her arms about his neck. 'Oh *yes*!' she glowed up at him. 'I love you, I love you, I love you!' She rained kisses all over his face and throat.

Adam laughed exultantly. 'I think you really love me,' he teased.

'Oh, I do!'

'Enough to marry me next week?'

'Enough to marry you whenever you want me to.'

His arms tightened. 'That would be now if I could arrange it. Unfortunately, I can't.'

'It doesn't matter.' She gazed up at him with love-filled eyes. 'Stay with me until we can be married.'

He was shaking his head before she had even finished speaking. 'I owe you a wedding night to remember, a legal wedding night,' he kissed her gently on the mouth, 'and I'm going to see to it that you get one. I've been such a fool about you, and all the time you were exactly what I thought you were, a beautiful and intelligent woman——'

'With a cold, calculating brain,' she teased.

'Don't!' he groaned. 'I don't enjoy being an idiot, and with you I seem to have been nothing else.'

Natalie lightly caressed his hard jaw. 'I seem to remember a few occasions when you were definitely something else,' she purred.

'Don't tempt me.' He put her firmly away from him. 'The next time I make love to you I'm going to have a gold wedding ring on your finger that's going to stay there for a lifetime!'

Natalie picked up the green receiver from the telephone as it began to ring, absently wrestling with the accounts, promising herself for the hundredth time that she would get herself professional help.

'Miss Faulkner?' a male voice demanded to know.

'Er——'

'Miss Faulkner, you and I have an appointment in half an hour,' the autocratic voice informed her. 'But I find I'm suddenly free now.'

Natalie smiled. 'I'll have to rearrange my schedule——'

'Then do so.' The line went dead.

She moved calmly, serenely, locking away the accounts, picking up her handbag before going into the outer office. 'I have to go out, Dee,' she told her secretary. 'Could you call Tracy and ask her to come in this afternoon instead of this morning?'

'I'll do that,' her friend nodded, grinning.

Natalie hummed to herself as she went out into the summer sunshine, unlocking her car to drive to her appointment. The lift seemed very slow as she took it up to the top floor, stepping straight into the lounge. Morton took her jacket, then quietly disappeared as Adam came through from the bedroom.

'I hope you realise that I had to cancel an appointment with Tracy,' she told him breathlessly, as always her senses beginning to spin just at the sight of him.

'I'm sure she won't mind.' He walked steadily towards her, his gaze firmly fixed on hers.

'She's doing very well as Fantasy Girl, isn't she?'

'Very well,' Adam curved her body into his. 'She's even started accepting the odd date.'

Tracy had been accepted world-wide as the Fantasy Girl. Her image was perfect, the hint of sadness in her eyes only adding to her mystery.

'I had a call from my parents this morning,' she told him. 'Judith and Jason are getting married.'

'They are?' He didn't seem particularly interested.

'Mm,' she nodded. 'Maybe they really do love each other.'

'Maybe.' He kissed her throat.

Judith and Jason had left for America only weeks after Jason's marriage had split up irrevocably. The fact that they were now going to get married must mean they felt genuine love for each other. As Natalie remembered Jason's furious statement about being obsessed with Judith she thought perhaps that wasn't so unlikely after all. Although she very much doubted the marriage would be tranquil and contented!

'You know why I had to see you?' Adam interrupted her wandering thoughts.

She smiled, gladly putting thoughts of her sister and Jason out of her mind, although she knew her parents were relieved that the relationship was going to be legalised, and shocked at their younger daughter's behaviour. 'I think I can guess,' Natalie grinned.

'I've been thinking about you all morning, darling.'

'It's only eleven o'clock!' she laughed mockingly.

'Three hours since I last made love to you!' Adam groaned. 'Come to bed.'

'Gladly!'

Afterwards she lay with her head on his shoulder, tracing patterns on his chest, loving the warm caress of his skin. Morton had become very adept at making himself scarce during the last ten months, and Natalie blushed as she realised just how much of that time she and Adam had spent in bed together.

'You'd better make the most of this,' she smiled up at him. 'Soon there won't be any lunchtimes spent in bed.'

'No.' Adam sat up to curve a hand round the contour of her stomach, her five months of pregnancy clearly showing in her otherwise slender body. 'There is just one thing——' He quirked one dark brow at her.

She was lazily relaxed and satiated, smiling. 'Yes?'

'I think the time has come to change the name of the agency,' he mocked. 'If I can call you "Miss Faulkner" and still get a response what must other people think when they see how very pregnant you are?'

'They must think I have a very virile lover!'

Adam chuckled. 'And instead you just have a sex-craved husband!'

'Yes,' she laughed with him. 'Besides, Adam

Thornton has the monopoly on enough things around here without including my agency.'

He rolled over and pinned her to the bed. 'Do I have the monopoly on you?' he sobered.

'Well, not any more.' She touched the hardness of his face. 'Your son or daughter will soon have a large chunk of me too.'

'If that's the only competition I ever have I won't mind,' and he began to kiss her.

Natalie marvelled at the passionate love she and Adam still felt for each other after almost a year of marriage. And soon they would have a child as a result of that love. Yes, perhaps now was the time to change the name of the agency to Thornton. She had so much. She was going to continue running the agency in an advisory capacity even when the baby had been born, with Dee taking over the management of it with the help of a young assistant.

Adam had given her everything—the pride of being his wife, the honour of giving him a child. And he had done it all without smothering her own sense of independence, making her bond to him all the stronger. Yes, Adam was a clever man, who knew her better than she knew herself, and he had bound her to him with a love that grew deeper as each day passed.

A FAMOUS ENGLISH MODEL

What better place for Natalie to operate a model agency than London, one of the world's fashion capitals! And English models have long been admired by the North American public—even before the Beatles landed on our shores and made everything English seem different and wonderful. One of the most famous English models, Twiggy, a scant ninety-one-pound teenager with a short boyish haircut and a lovely face, rode the crest of the American craze for things British.

This skinny London girl wasn't always chased by photographers. Although she dreamed of being a fashion model (she always carried with her a photograph of her idol, beautiful English model Jean Shrimpton), Lesley Hornby once described herself as having been very plain as a young girl, with freckles, crooked front teeth—later straightened—and long limp hair. Yet, however unlikely it seemed, Twiggy was to become a star. Taken under the wing of her boyfriend-manager—who nicknamed her Twiggy—she was relentlessly promoted in Britain as a different "look." In the fall of 1966, seventeen-year-old Twiggy burst into international prominence, rivaling even her adored Shrimpton. Twiggy's waiflike figure appeared on the covers of major magazines, crowds followed her while she toured the United States, and everywhere people were buying Twiggy dolls, makeup, T-shirts, pens and false eyelashes.

After a few years the fad died down. Twiggy married, had children and even put on weight...but women the world over are still striving for even a shadow of that glamorous sixties' thinness Twiggy inspired.

Yours FREE, with a home subscription to SUPERROMANCE™

Now you never have to miss reading the newest **SUPERROMANCES**... because they'll be delivered right to your door.

Start with your **FREE** LOVE BEYOND DESIRE. You'll be enthralled by this powerful love story...from the moment Robin meets the dark, handsome Carlos and finds herself involved in the jealousies, bitterness and secret passions of the Lopez family. Where her own forbidden love threatens to shatter her life.

Your **FREE** LOVE BEYOND DESIRE is only the beginning. A subscription to **SUPERROMANCE** lets you look forward to a long love affair. Month after month, you'll receive four love stories of heroic dimension. Novels that will involve you in spellbinding intrigue, forbidden love and fiery passions.

You'll begin this series of sensuous, exciting contemporary novels...written by some of the top romance novelists of the day...with four every month.

And this big value...each novel, almost 400 pages of compelling reading...is yours for only $2.50 a book. Hours of entertainment every month for so little. Far less than a first-run movie or pay-TV. Newly published novels, with beautifully illustrated covers, filled with page after page of delicious escape into a world of romantic love...delivered right to your home.

Begin a long love affair with

SUPERROMANCE.

Accept LOVE BEYOND DESIRE, **FREE.**

Complete and mail the coupon below, today!

- -

FREE! Mail to: SUPERROMANCE

In the U.S.
1440 South Priest Drive
Tempe, AZ 85281

In Canada
649 Ontario St.
Stratford, Ontario N5A 6W2

YES, please send me FREE and without any obligation, my **SUPERROMANCE** novel, LOVE BEYOND DESIRE. If you do not hear from me after I have examined my FREE book, please send me the 4 new **SUPERROMANCE** books every month as soon as they come off the press. I understand that I will be billed only $2.50 for each book (total $10.00). There are no shipping and handling or any other hidden charges. There is no minimum number of books that I have to purchase. In fact, I may cancel this arrangement at any time. LOVE BEYOND DESIRE is mine to keep as a FREE gift, even if I do not buy any additional books.

NAME _____ (Please Print)

ADDRESS _____ APT. NO. _____

CITY _____

STATE/PROV. _____ ZIP/POSTAL CODE _____

SIGNATURE (If under 18, parent or guardian must sign.)

This offer is limited to one order per household and not valid to present subscribers. Prices subject to change without notice. Offer expires
Offer expires January 31, 1984   PR307

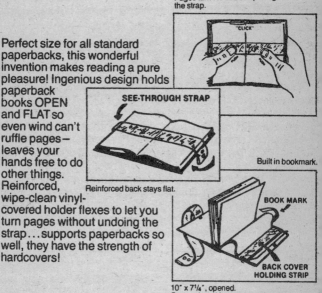

Enter a uniquely exciting world of romance with the new

Harlequin American Romances.™

Harlequin American Romances are the first romances to explore today's new love relationships. These compelling romance novels reach into the hearts and minds of women across North America...probing the most intimate moments of romance, love and desire.

You'll follow romantic heroines and irresistible men as they boldly face confusing choices. Career first, love later? Love without marriage? Long-distance relationships? All the experiences that make love real are captured in the tender, loving pages of the new **Harlequin American Romances.**

What makes North American women so different when it comes to love? Find out in the new **Harlequin American Romances!**

Send for your introductory FREE book now!

AR-SUB-2